What People Are Saying About

The Quietist

Gothard has Siri Hustvedt's exquisite gift for characterisation, and he deftly navigates the reader through the myriad treasures and pains that result from intimacy.
Guy Mankowski

Daniel Gothard paints an honest, raw picture of the way adult relationships both begin and end.
Liz Loves Books **blog**

An entertaining and thought-provoking novel that uses traditional virtues of storytelling to portray the complexity of modern existence.
Mike Fox, Nightjar Press

The Quietist

A Novel

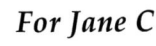

The Quietist

A Novel

by Daniel David Gothard

ROUNDFIRE
BOOKS

London, UK
Washington, DC, USA

CollectiveInk

First published by Roundfire Books, 2025
Roundfire Books is an imprint of Collective Ink Ltd.,
Unit 11, Shepperton House, 89 Shepperton Road, London, N1 3DF
office@collectiveinkbooks.com
www.collectiveinkbooks.com
www.roundfire-books.com

For distributor details and how to order please visit the 'Ordering' section on our website.

Text copyright: Daniel David Gothard 2024

ISBN: 978 1 80341 885 8
978 1 80341 892 6 (ebook)
Library of Congress Control Number: 2024939935

All rights reserved. Except for brief quotations in critical articles or reviews, no part of this book may be reproduced in any manner without prior written permission from the publishers.

The rights of Daniel David Gothard as author have been asserted in accordance with the Copyright, Designs and Patents Act 1988.

A CIP catalogue record for this book is available from the British Library.

Design: Lapiz Digital Services

UK: Printed and bound by CPI Group (UK) Ltd, Croydon, CR0 4YY
Printed in North America by CPI GPS partners

We operate a distinctive and ethical publishing philosophy in all areas of our business, from our global network of authors to production and worldwide distribution.

Quietism: *(noun)* — *Calm acceptance of things as they are without attempts to resist or change them.*

A memory suddenly recalled. A patch of breath clouding the bottom-middle of the car window next to a cold cheek. There is a heart in the patch. The heart has been poorly drawn by an index finger and a misaligned arrow skewers it.

Four letters are written in the heart:

H A T E.

The heart fades and the memory cuts like a film scene into a spin of images — the countryside and variety of car types going by become a whirl of instantly seen and forgotten blur as the vehicle feels more like a bumper car in a loud fairground.

The sounds of screeching and collapsing metal, of tyre explosions, of screaming are gone as if the volume of all life has been turned to zero. A low wheeze. A warm liquid runs down the centre of a nose and drips from the end. A neck is aching.

Sirens are coming.

1

It took Patrick Hawton a long time to get rid of the metallic taste after the motorway pile-up that killed his wife and twenty-seven other people.

He managed to forget the sounds and sight of death reasonably quickly on being discharged from hospital, but the taste in his mouth served as a constant reminder that something had been lost and he had to find it again.

'Loss and realising exactly what has gone from your life can take a long time to come out in each person, Patrick. You shouldn't feel bad because you haven't cried yet or begun to feel the worst of it. You are in severe shock', the psychiatrist, Doctor Lanning, at the hospital, had said, more than once. In fact he seemed to labour the subject of severe shock and how Patrick would reach an emotional catalyst, somewhere in his recovery, when the gush of feelings and suppressed thoughts would break free like an exploded dam.

The mind doctor was in his mid-fifties. He had a short greying beard and thinning hair and looked overworked. Patrick found himself not listening to Lanning's words. He felt so calm and relaxed in his bed and was happy to let his mind wander freely, pretending interest and answering questions as he thought he should: *Yes, he missed his wife. Yes, he felt amazed he had survived. And, no, he couldn't remember what had happened just prior to the crash.*

Patrick looked into Lanning's eyes and wondered about his existence outside the hospital, whether he was married, for how long, happily or trapped in an empty shell? Perhaps he had had patients who had fallen in love with him, had he had affairs? Did he have any children, and if so did they still talk to him regularly or had he alienated them through years of analytical insights, which had been meant generously, as gentle parental nudges towards a healthy mental life. But maybe he had found himself, too late in life to start afresh, left alone by those he had held too close for so long; all his expertise on the how and why people do things may have amounted to nothing, and here he found himself, in another patient's hospital room, called in to offer trauma counselling to one of only three survivors from the disaster. Did Patrick's lack of emotion sicken Lanning? Did the psychiatrist want to lean across the arm of the chair next to Patrick's bed and whisper, 'You really are a cold person. Repressed and cold.'

Perhaps, when Lanning talked about the depths of loss, he was talking about himself.

'Do you have any mints or chewing gum, Doctor Lanning?' Patrick said.

Lanning's eyes widened as if Patrick had just come to some conclusive decision and provided a psychological revelation.

'Sorry, what?'

'Mints ... or gum? I still have this awful taste in my mouth as if I swallowed a chunk of metal and its wedged in my soft palate, eroding bit by bit, and leaving me with a continual taste.'

'Er, no. Sorry. I'll pop to the ground-floor shop in a minute and buy you some. Which would you prefer?'

'Extra-strong, please. Thanks.'

'May I just ask you about your wife, before I get the mints?'

'Of course. What would you like to know about her?'

Patrick sat up in bed, his left arm was bandaged and a bit sore. He habitually tried resting it on the bar of the bedside and each time pulled it away with a momentary wince.

'How long had you been married?'

'Six years, just over six.'

'Do you remember being happy with her?'

'What do you mean exactly by "happy"? Do you mean happy just before the crash or happy in a general way?'

1

Lanning thought for a moment and then shrugged. 'Do you have a sense of being happy with her? Do you have that feeling about your marriage or not?' he said.

Patrick wondered if this was a standard psychiatrist trick, to take a subject as wide-ranging as happiness and all its different varieties of time, place, situation and the rest, and reduce it to a single concept. Or maybe Lanning couldn't be bothered to stretch his mind on this issue, and was desperate to think of the next point of analysis, find something to talk about; they still had ten minutes of their daily session left, this was their eighth.

They hadn't really talked about the death of Patrick's wife, Maggie, before now and the only previous mention of the marriage was during the first session, when Lanning confirmed some personal details with Patrick.

'Happiness is such a difficult thing to remember, isn't it? Difficult to feel in the moment, too. I mean you can summon days, events, images of moments perhaps, those which might symbolise happiness in your life, but to remember something as ephemeral as the feeling itself, especially in a marriage ... I'm not sure I can really say for certain. Sorry,' Patrick said. He sat up straight and smiled at Lanning, who returned the gesture with the additional look of a concerned friend.

'Sorry is a word you never have to use with me, Patrick. I'm just curious about your relationship with Maggie ... do you mind me using her name?'

'Of course not, that's fine.'

'Good, good. Some people, after the kind of tragedy you've suffered, can't even bring themselves to hear or speak the name of someone they've lost. It's a big step for you to do that and begin the process of talking about her.'

There was a moment of silence. Lanning wrote something down and Patrick looked at the Escher painting on the wall at the end of the bed — stairs overlapping stairs, the endless journey that might lead the traveller out of their minds. Had it been put there to make Patrick think about the crash, to open *his* mind to his new world and recalibrate his life. How could a painting as frustrating as that ever help the wounded?

'Doctor Lanning?' Patrick said; he coughed and took a sip of water.

'Yes, Patrick.'

'I don't want to bother you, but I was wondering if, as the session's almost over, you would buy those mints for me, please?'

'Oh yes, yes, of course.'

Lanning stood quickly, brushed his trousers as if they were covered in crumbs, as he always did, and put his pad and pen on the armchair. He put both hands in his trouser pockets, nodded in recognition of finding some small change, smiled at Patrick and walked out.

The psychiatrist stopped to use the public toilet. He used a cubicle, his white coat and hospital identification badge brought on occasional, and always unwanted, conversations. Lanning stood up straight, watching his light yellow flow of urine trickle to nothing and thought of the ever-present expression on Patrick Hawton's face, an expression of bewildered expectation and hope. How the hell could the man have retained *any* hope, even in the cage of shock he was obviously contained inside after the crash?

Lanning washed his hands like a surgeon, fingernails on the palms, ten rubs on both sides of both hands, watching the suds pop and grow between his fingers. He used a pocket of his white coat to open the toilet door; so many men didn't wash their hands and the hideous microbiological possibilities had, over so many years, provoked the mysophobic out of his character. He looked up and down the corridor and walked to the small shop nearby. He looked at the mint and chewing gum selection, thought of how nasty the continuous taste of metal in a mouth must be and picked up three packets of extra-strong mints.

1

'There you are. I hope these help. I suppose the taste difference will be fairly short-lived, but it's something. Perhaps I should speak to the nurses, there may be a mouthwash, something with longer lasting power', Lanning said as he handed the sweets to Patrick, who was smiling as if he had been visited by an angel of mercy.

In moments of seeming beatification such as this, Lanning wanted to ask Patrick what was going through his mind, the exactitude of his thinking. Was he faking such adoration in his gratitude? Was he glad to be alive? Or was there some underlying neurological issue that would manifest later on in his treatments and prove to be his psychological downfall?

'All right, Patrick, that's it for today. Do you have any questions for me?'

Lanning knew the answer before he asked the question.

'No, that's great, doctor. And thanks for the mints.'

'My pleasure. I'll see you tomorrow. And if you need to talk to me, any time, ask one of the nurses to call me. Try and rest.'

Lanning and Patrick nodded goodbyes at each other and the psychiatrist left.

While Lanning had been off buying the mints, Patrick had wanted to look at the notepad left on the armchair. He had been wanting to read the session notes for some time, but his broken right ankle, almost healed now, had previously prevented him. He wondered what the man-of-the-mind thought of him. Did he think Patrick was insane — driven to that point by the trauma aftermath — because he didn't exhibit any visible signs of psychological or emotional agony?

The constant talk of shock, severe or not, how did Lanning know Patrick *was* in shock? Surely being in a state of shock was the lack of realising your situation, being oblivious to changes, pain, loss. Patrick understood his new life: Maggie was dead, lots of other people too. He was in hospital and soon enough he would have to begin his reality outside the ward.

And that was all right with Patrick, that was what life was all about, the beginnings, middles, and always the endings.

The notepad had been lying, waiting for Patrick to slope out of his bed and reach across. Surely it was his right to know that information?

But before he could manage the effort, the Escher stairs had caught his eye again. Something was moving on those stairs, a woman with her back to him.

Patrick had looked down at his feet and felt the cold of the stone beneath him, all around were more stairs: his bed, the ward, everything he had been so confined by had disappeared and he was walking up, higher and higher, and then around a corner, to one side and finally spiralling until he saw the woman again — her back still to him. He began calling out, but stopped, thinking of the myth of Orpheus and Eurydice, the underworld, this journey, and he was struck dumb by the sense that if this woman stopped and looked back he would lose something.

The bong of the patient-assist bell on the ward made him smile at Lanning as he returned with the mints. Patrick glanced at the Escher picture a last time before feeling the melt of the first sweet in his mouth, a temporary but highly welcome change to that awful metal taste.

He had often thought about being single again, that much he could remember, although he would never tell Lanning that secret, it would almost certainly mean hour upon hour of deepened analysis. And lead nowhere. He didn't want to think about some of the new ideas coming in to his head throughout the days in bed, but he couldn't stop them, and had decided to let every thought — however immediately absurd or repugnant — wash over him. He could file and remember the good stuff and dump the rest.

Patrick *knew* he would never have wanted anything bad to happen to Maggie, regardless of his lack of happy memories. He knew he felt real love when he thought of her and not some

1

post-tragedy-manufactured love. He remembered them getting married, how her naked body felt against him after lovemaking, 'I love you, Patty, my Pat,' Maggie sometimes said after sex, like a mantra.

He remembered the smell of her freshly washed hair. But none of those memories made him sad — was that part of Lanning's *severe shock status*? He had a photograph of Maggie next to his bed. His sister, Celia, had brought that in for him, she visited Patrick every afternoon after her work.

'Are you certain you want to be reminded of the pain so soon?' Celia had asked.

Celia worked in advertising and was used to fast answers and quick-fire solutions, the world in black and white. She liked short messages that sold concepts, and not just clothing and cars, but in life itself. She was given, at family meals, to answering questions in short bursts of adjectives; nothing that could resemble a sentence, just a series of billboard-style memes that the recipient of the 'answer' was supposed to be enlightened by.

Patrick had always previously thought of her as highly efficient, but in the last couple of weeks one of the many new inclinations that might seem unlikely and unkind was of distancing himself from her when he was discharged.

'I want to feel as if she's still with me', Patrick had lied. Sometimes when he concentrated on her face — her lips, her shiny eyes — there was an avalanche of new concepts, angles on living without her and technicolour philosophical possibilities that followed, and Patrick had thought everything would become more distinct and linear with an actual image of his dead wife to stare at. This was still new, but talking to her photo helped him think about the next part of his life, the one without her.

2

Lanning closed his office door and sat at his desk. He unbuttoned his coat and unscrewed the top of his bottle of water. The cool liquid in his mouth pooled for a few seconds and allowed the psychiatrist a ponderous moment to think straight; analytical sessions with trauma patients always made him feel tense, as if, even after so many years doing this work, he still might say something to exacerbate the mental pain. And as he swallowed the mouthful he reached for Patrick's file. Medical records were computerised now, but Lanning kept hard-copy notes and had been sent photographs of the crash scene by the transport police.

'Christ almighty', Lanning whispered, staring at the hideous images. Even though he had seen them all before it was still a shock to witness the crush and rip of the human anatomy in a high impact incident.

An image of the dead Maggie came in to focus, slumped on an airbag, bunched up as if her bones had been removed. 'I hope he *doesn't* remember everything. I wonder whether he saw her in that state?'

He closed the file and put it in the top drawer of his desk. The psychiatrist had conferred with two colleagues about the efficacy of showing some of the less horrific photographs to Patrick, as a way — a mental bridge — in to his memories, as part of the recovery process. But the colleagues had both thought it was too early in the treatment planning, that such a push could, potentially, create a catatonic positioning of Patrick's thoughts and send his psyche so deep inside the darkest recesses of his brain that he might never lead a normal life again. And that plainly wasn't a risk worth taking.

Lanning made himself a cup of tea and began typing up his notes from the earlier session with Patrick:

2

It is my opinion the patient, Patrick Hawton, is still in a state of complete shock, so severe that he appears oblivious to the tremendous levels of change and trauma he has experienced. As in all our previous sessions, Patrick provides me with relevant information and is highly congenial, but his total lack of awareness, immediate memory recall and an inability to express even the most basic of painful thoughts is a clear sign that he still has a long way to go towards any level of psychological balance. He is suffering from a massive aftermath of post-traumatic stress disorder and it is my recommendation that I continue to treat him on a daily basis.

Lanning stopped, took a long sip of tea from his flask cup, and wondered about adding medication suggestions to the notes. Patrick was currently being prescribed painkillers and some antibiotics for a leg infection, but nothing for his mind. Lanning thought of going further in relation to the photographs again and positing the idea of pushing Patrick with details, questions, challenging facts, incrementally harder and harder each day to face his tragedy. But psychiatry and tough love compressed into one mix was a risky business and nobody wanted the worst outcome for the patient, or a familial lawsuit for malpractice. Lanning knew he had a case worth following, that there was a deeper reason and purpose about Patrick and his consequential behaviour — this might even become something he could publish in the *Journal of Psychiatry* to re-establish his credentials. Lanning had felt like a dinosaur in his discipline for years. He could do *good*, help Patrick back to the permanence of reality and provide him with the self-knowledge and tools for a future. Surely that was his duty? And his opportunity.

Lanning saved his notes and closed the file, finished his tea and went to lunch.

3

Two weeks later, halfway through a psychiatric session, Patrick sat up suddenly, as if he had been sleeping and awoken by a nightmare, and said to Lanning, 'I have two questions for you, doctor.'

Lanning had been making a note relating to the vacant expression on Patrick's face, something that had become more and more pronounced in recent days, something which, at first, Lanning had assumed was boredom or fatigue. But now he was beginning to think it could be something much worse. And he would research his idea more later that day.

'Yes, Patrick.'

'The first question is, do I *have* to stay in the hospital now? Is there any further clinical reason for me to stay? And the second is, how are the other two survivors doing, have they been discharged?'

The psychiatrist adjusted his sitting position and breathed out.

'Well, as far as I know, there isn't any *critical* need for you to stay. I'll be honest about this. I have asked that your stay be extended a while for us to continue our work, and I believe your consultant was a bit worried about your blood pressure and cortisol levels. However, I can check with him and we can talk about a departure date if you like?'

Patrick grinned and nodded.

'Oh yeah, please. I have *so* many plans for life outside this place. I mean, don't get me wrong, everyone, you especially, has been wonderful, but I feel as if I'm going a bit stir-crazy.' Patrick poured the words out like an overdosing caffeine addict.

'Well, all right. What I would like to suggest, and I would like you to consider this *very* carefully, is that even after you've been discharged we keep a weekly session ongoing. How does that sound?'

Lanning expected procrastination.

'Sure. Absolutely. That's exactly what I'd like', Patrick said, his voice raised like a winner of some prize. 'And would you be able to answer my second question, about the other two crash survivors? I don't even know their names.'

This wasn't true. Patrick had seen enough news footage to know virtually all the public domain information about the motorway crash: Ian McInnerny and Catherine Stannard were the names of the other *lucky* ones.

'That's very good news about the session work. As to the health and treatment of the other survivors, I'm really sorry, Patrick, I can't discuss that with anyone, other than another medical professional connected to their cases. Sorry.'

Ian McInnerny had died a week earlier after a massive, undetected, cerebral haemorrhage. But Catherine Stannard was recovering well and was due to be discharged within the next couple of days. She had lost her partner in the crash, and there was a part of Lanning's treatment plan which included the possibility of introducing she and Patrick at some future point, carefully and in a very secure environment. Some research in the United States had showed pleasing results in the group share experience of those who had been through the same disaster and survived.

'That's a shame. I'd like to know more about them. I feel as if we have a connection now ... a kind of symbiotic relationship. Does that make sense?'

Patrick knew Ian McInnerny was dead. He was interested in Catherine Stannard.

Lanning smiled — this might be a breakthrough moment.

'It makes perfect sense, Patrick, perfect sense.'

On the day of Patrick's discharge he had woken early, showered, packed his clothing and washbag, and had been sitting ready to leave as the breakfast cart arrived just after 7 o'clock.

Doctor Lanning was also in the hospital early that day — both Patrick and Catherine Stannard were being discharged on the same day and he wanted to make certain his file notes were complete and that both patients were aware of his continuing physical presence in their lives.

4

'So, Catherine, your father is collecting you, is that correct?' Lanning said. He sat across the room from her, both of them sipping coffee. Lanning thought Catherine looked transformed physically from her admittance, when she was badly slashed across the forehead and her right arm was bent backwards, broken in five places; she had remained unconscious for two days. And now her body was fixed she was very pretty, although Lanning would only allow himself a momentary acknowledgment of that fact, but her eyes looked full of grief.

'Yeah, my dad should be here fairly soon.' Catherine looked at her wristwatch and smiled at Lanning.

'Are you going to leave all the cards and flowers behind?'

Catherine looked surprised for a moment, turned and stared at the display of GET WELL SOON items covering the bedside table and walls behind her — balloons, cards, flowers, all the well-meaning thoughts — and then turned back to Lanning.

'I'm well now, physically better anyway. I don't want to be reminded of any of what...'

Lanning leaned forward and quietly said, 'I understand. If it feels right, do it that way.'

Catherine's eyes began to fill with tears, her jaw set in defiance against her feelings. She wiped them away quickly, as if she wouldn't allow herself any more public displays of bereavement.

Lanning sat up straight, finished his coffee and decided to force a productive atmosphere into the room.

'So, although this probably isn't the best time to ask you about my ongoing therapy idea, I just want to see if you've given any thought to continuing to have a weekly session with me. I appreciate you were hesitant at first, which is completely understandable, but...'

Catherine interrupted Lanning, 'I would like to keep coming in, yes. I need to get this feeling out of me, doctor. I know I can't live in the past, especially a past filled with sounds and memories of death. It still feels so present. I keep hearing the squeal of the tyres before the impact, and looking over at Harry's face.'

Catherine closed her eyes and let her head drop for a moment. Then she looked up, forced a smile and sipped some more coffee.

Lanning smiled and compared this remarkable, emotionally honest young woman with Patrick's robot-like demeanour. And then he made a decision.

'There is one last thing I would really like you to think about, give serious consideration to. The only other survivor is also being discharged today and he has agreed to see me on a weekly basis too. I honestly believe the two of you would benefit from some form of shared therapy, not every week, but perhaps one or two sessions of open dialogue about the now, and how what happened has changed you.'

Catherine looked less than enthusiastic.

'I don't know, doctor, that makes me feel odd, like some kind of intrusion.' Catherine sat forward and looked directly into Lanning's eyes. 'The thought of meeting the only other survivor, I don't really know about that. I have this image in my mind of being the one who made it through the crash, the only one with distinct thoughts and visions and feelings about it, as if ... as if I couldn't accept anybody telling me *their* story in case it contradicted something I had experienced. Does that make sense at all?'

'It does, completely. There is always a very personal, almost intimate, dimension to any tragedy, however large or small, however many survivors there are. I wouldn't ask you to even think about doing this unless I was convinced of its probable benefits for both of you.'

4

A man appeared at Catherine's doorway, and by the way she smiled at him, Lanning knew it was her father. The two men introduced themselves and shook hands.

'I will think about what you've suggested, doctor. I take what you say very seriously. You've been great and helped me so much. Thank you.'

Catherine shook his hand, and then hugged the psychiatrist. Lanning felt her tremble. And then she was walking away with her family.

Catherine watched the hospital disappear behind her, her first time in a car since the accident. She closed her eyes for a moment, saw the same image in her mind of Harry smiling at her just before the slam and twist of the accident, the sun behind his head. He had looked like an angel then and perhaps he was one now. But what good was an angel to her? She had nothing to live for now and was happier thinking she could be with Harry again soon.

She had lied and placated Lanning, telling him all the things she had guessed, correctly, he wanted to hear during their sessions: about how she had come to terms with the tragedy and loss, and how she felt she *could* start again.

She thought about the motorway every day, the details, the slow-motion playback in her mind, a sudden jolt of her body forwards and then on to Harry's shoulder; they had banged heads with each other. There was the screaming all around, men and women connected by extreme terror, the smashing of windows, the deafening blast of bending and breaking iron, her eyes blinking away the blood pouring from her forehead, her arm in so much pain she could barely scream herself. And finally, just before she had passed out, she had looked at Harry one last time — his eyes were dull, a grey film covered them, nothing behind; his soul had risen away. She knew that last vision of her lover was him in death, a mask over the vital man she had planned to marry.

She hadn't gotten rid of the hole in her guts, the sense that she was rotting from the inside out and that she would eventually combust into the Rapture. She knew her soul was shrivelled and groaning into dust.

Catherine presumed Lanning was probably feeling very satisfied with his treatment of her; perhaps he was in his office right at that moment, preening himself in the small mirror above his desk, checking his teeth for breakfast muesli or combing his hair — a job well done, he might think.

His words and questions had always felt so practiced and textbook-friendly, as if she wasn't an individual case at all, but merely another file in his computer to be processed through the health system: *patch 'em up and ship 'em out...*

But Catherine *was* intrigued by the other survivor, and in that much, Lanning had succeeded. Would she recognise this person from the motorway, the ambulances being loaded?

Catherine couldn't find any solution for the question that kept going through her head, insistent and angry in its nag: *How was she supposed to trudge through all the rest of her days feeling like this?* It was all too hard to deal with, even sitting next to her adoring father, who she adored right back. He was trying to make conversation with her, doing his best to bring her back into a world she might recognise, telling recent, innocuous anecdotes about her brother and mother. But Catherine could tell he was nervous by the way he kept glancing at her as if she might open her seatbelt and fly out of the window next to her. There weren't any obvious reasons to live, no vengeance for her to enact, no compensation to be gained from any negligent authority.

She was *empty* and she knew she would probably stay that way. But if there was any hope for her it might be within the seed of this idea of Lanning's — shared experience therapy. She might find a kindred spirit, something good that had remained trapped inside those crumpled cars, lorries and coaches. And so she *would* go on, at least for as long as the sessions lasted, she would give life a very last chance. But, as her father laughed to himself about the family dog still not understanding the difference between sit, lie down and shake paws, she made a promise that if she didn't regain any motivation to continue her earthbound journey in a post-therapy world, she would find her wings and join Harry.

5

Patrick's sister insisted on following him into his home. She closed the front door very carefully, as if she might disturb some part of his previous life with any sort of touch or vibration.

'Thanks, Celia. I really appreciate the lift. I should be okay from here.'

'I'll get you some shopping. What would you like?'

Celia looked at her phone and typed something into it. She looked up at Patrick and raised her eyebrows, smiled, then gave him a look of affectionate pity.

Your face changes as quickly as your slogans, Patrick thought.

'I'm okay. I've got things in the freezer and cupboards and there's always a takeaway', he said, smiling back but wanting her to leave.

'Okay, but I will make us some tea.'

'Really, Celia. It's all right. I'll be fine. You get back to work and I'll call you if I need anything.'

Celia turned the corners of her mouth down, reminding Patrick of awful paintings of sad clowns, then stepped forward and hugged him. Her arms were thin and uncomfortable, her elbows dug into him, and it was the first human contact he had had since Maggie died. He froze and stared at a cobweb in the corner of the lounge ceiling. It swung and lifted, partially drooping on to the novels on the highest shelf below. Patrick noticed three Margaret Atwood books he hadn't thought of for a long time.

'Always listen to a Margaret', Maggie had said after finishing *The Handmaid's Tale*. 'Apart from the Thatcher kind.'

'I'll check in with you tonight. Call if you need me', Celia shouted from the hallway. She closed the front door even more carefully.

Don't wake the dead, Patrick thought.

6

Lanning sat in his small study and began to re-read all of Catherine and Patrick's session notes. The process took him three hours and by the time he finished he was certain he wouldn't have a clue where to start shared therapy sessions. The notes reminded him of the questionnaires he had written for the hospital when he arrived there to start his job, sixteen years ago. He had felt confident then his basic enquiries to anybody needing his counselling would be more than enough to elicit the necessary information for him to form a treatment profile. But that was then. He needed so much more to begin this new process, added to which he hadn't spoken to the hospital administration about any legal liabilities they might be open to, or to any colleagues in the department about the ethical boundaries involved. What the hell am I doing, he thought, I'm an old fraud who doesn't know where to start or what to say. I could easily ruin two lives.

Lanning sat back and looked at the mess on his desk. Three empty mugs, two with tea stains, one with coffee dregs. There were books on the floor and the bin needed emptying. It was eight months since Jane had died and he had used that time to find ways to rebuild any solid reputation he had previously felt in his job. The house had become a place to sleep, eat and leave as soon as he could each morning.

'I really think you should be with us for a little while', Catherine's father said. He sipped his tea and didn't look at her. 'It seems too soon to leave you alone.'

Catherine looked at the photograph of herself and Harry, dressed in smart clothing, at Harry's sister's wedding, two years ago. That will be the closest we'll come to a day like that, she thought. What was the point of all the time spent making plans, building a relationship, the emotion invested, if it was all for nothing in the end? Was it *really* better to have loved and lost than to have not loved at all?

'I'll be just fine. I need to get used to being mostly alone, and I think it might be good for me. The hospital was intense and uncomfortable. I want my home comforts back. Please try not to worry', Catherine said to her father, who was smiling at her. He nodded and looked resigned to having no say in his daughter's life.

'That doctor seemed like a nice chap', Catherine's father said.

Catherine nodded and sipped her tea, remembering Lanning's face and his last words before she left, '... *probable benefits for both of you*'. She wanted to see who the other survivor was, what he looked like, what he felt now, what he had lost, did he want to go on or just come to the inevitable end they both escaped from on the motorway. Was this all fate? She didn't believe in that. And was Lanning the right person to piece it all together for them. He seemed professional and intelligent, but there was something jaded about the way he talked to her, the way he seemed engaged one moment and going through the therapeutic motions the next. Did he have anything to offer them, other than coffee, biscuits and a reassuring smile after they had opened their hearts? The risk seemed to be outweighing the potential benefits Lanning had mentioned, by quite a lot.

7

Patrick dreamed a lot about Maggie. She was never particularly distinct. Never stopping long enough for him to look at her face. Her long, thick red hair seem determined to cover her every possible expression and there were never any moments to hold her still and really gaze at her features. Perhaps she didn't want him to see how she had looked after the accident? He tried saying something to her, in each dream, but everything was unclear and reactive, unrecognisable faces appearing in each dream, those who tried to keep them apart, then jump-cuts to different settings and scenes he couldn't understand. Those frenetic nights ended in the early hours as the sun was illuminating the edges of his bedroom curtains. Maggie had chosen them. He looked at the thin cotton now and realised that was one of many changes he could make. He went to the bathroom each morning and looked at the diagonal creases above each of his eyebrows, embedded from the deepest sleeping focus and concentration. His eyes often looked sore from being rubbed. He wondered if that was a result of crying or disbelief, that he had seen something, in amongst the blur and frenzy, which indicated reason and solution, something which told him the truth about his departed love, its death and afterwards.

8

Lanning took a long time deciding how far apart the two chairs should be from each other, and from him. He had arrived at the hospital two hours before the first shared therapy appointment with Catherine and Patrick, drunk a large cup of horrible coffee and tried to get rid of the aftertaste with two of the extra-strong mints he had in his desk drawer, from a packet he had forgotten to give to Patrick.

Was it a good idea to position them on the other side of the door to his office, with their backs to the wall? That might present the feeling they were trapped, on trial with nowhere to go. He placed the chairs with their backs to the door and his with the back next to the window. That was an awful choice. It would probably make them feel distracted by the view behind him and, potentially, vulnerable to someone coming into the room without them noticing and overhearing their most private and painful thoughts and memories. How close should their chairs be? Perhaps he should place them a good distance apart, with his in the middle? But that might feel as if the session was a debate and he was just a moderator. If their chairs were too close, they might feel as if he was attempting to force a quick bond between them, that might alienate them from any form of emotional honesty and shut the whole idea down from the start. Should he sit behind his desk? No, no, no. That would feel like an interview.

'Oh my god', he said, kicking one of the chairs over. 'Why don't I suggest we all stand on one foot and hop around the room.'

Lanning settled on placing the three chairs in the middle of his floor, his facing the wall, the other two facing his desk. Catherine and Patrick would be around two metres apart and he put a coffee table between them, to rest their drinks on and to make them feel as if there was a comfortable and secure boundary of sorts. In that way, neither of them would be distracted by the far away tree lines or the possibility of unwanted attention from the doorway. As close to a happy compromise as he could imagine and manage at that point. He took one last look at the set-up before leaving his room to use the toilet. Lanning had taken his nail-clippers with him and, after scrubbing his hands and checking his teeth, used them to trim his fingernails down to virtually nothing. A surgeon friend of his had explained the microbiological horrors of bacteria getting caught around cuticles and that had changed the way Lanning saw his place of work forever, a massive Petri dish just waiting to infect him. He adjusted his tie, then took it off, checking to see if the more casual, open collar look might suit the atmosphere of sharing more, literally being more open. No, the tie was the most professional approach. He was the one leading them and he needed to look as if he knew what he was doing.

Lanning stared at himself in the large bathroom mirror. The glass was flecked with soapy water splash marks. They clung to areas around the reflection of the middle of his face. He squinted and made his nose look sharper by forcing the skin on the bridge downwards and making it tighter. He raised his right eyebrow and pushed it as high as it would go. He finished his attempt at The Serious Professional styling by sucking his cheekbones in a bit. He looked at himself, side to side then full face-on, and was reminded of his father, old and angry. But his resting face looked so soft and anxious and scared. He would have to put his ego to one side for as long as this process might take.

The first sign of possible error in his forward therapy planning was already showing — he hadn't told anyone about the shared element. He had meant to inform the senior hospital management, but decided against it. They were pen-pushers not clinical staff. They wouldn't understand and would, almost certainly, tell him not to go outside the boundaries of agreed practice. Freud and Jung hadn't served agreed practice; none of the most radical and successful therapy ever emerged from that level of safe and unhelpful mundanity.

He had toyed with the idea of consulting Jim Henry, a psychiatrist friend from the university, but even his potential approbation would simply confirm what Lanning *knew*. He was doing the right thing for his patients, absolutely. They were under his care and this was their treatment plan.

Lanning walked back to his office, stopping for a few moments to look out of the head-height rectangular windows at the two massive hospital chimneys. He didn't know what they were for but had wanted to imagine them as being connected to the laundry unit and not the morgue. The floors had been waxed and washed, and the corridors outside the wards were usually empty and quiet. The only downsides to this place were the smells and the patients he didn't treat. As he approached his own corridor he noticed a sitting figure in the waiting area of his unit. It was Patrick. He was early.

'Patrick, hello', Lanning said. This was his usual greeting but he wasn't feeling full of salutations. He was annoyed he was probably being pushed to begin a pre-session by one of two patients, perhaps give a pep-talk or be calmly coerced to pass on some information about Catherine. This felt intolerable. Lanning had wanted, needed, some time alone to gather his thoughts, have another cup of the horrible coffee, or two, and be allowed to read his notes again; build himself up to the biggest challenge of his career. He wanted to tell Patrick to take a walk or find a cup of something warm, sit somewhere else. Lanning would have to invite him into the office, rather than imagine hearing him breathing just outside the door. But that would destabilise his *new* approach, his *new* method plan. To allow Patrick in early might ruin the shared therapy before it even began.

'My apologies for being so early. I couldn't sleep and I thought I would get dressed and walk here. It didn't take long at all.'

'That's perfectly all right, Patrick. You never need to apologise. Would you like to come in?'

Lanning made a gesture towards his office. He knew it was more of a finger flick than a guiding palm.

'I haven't seen your office before today', Patrick said, as thoughtfully as someone who is making a series of decisions that may have great consequence. 'Are they all the same ... the offices in this unit, I mean?'

Lanning poured the first of two cups of coffee, thinking how he might need to make more for the session. Should he start making it now? No, he was too distracted. Why did Patrick have to do this today?

He closed and reopened his eyes, tightly then wide, trying to imagine how he would be able to make small talk as the seconds went by until Catherine's arrival. He glanced at his wristwatch, that was still around forty-five minutes away.

'I suppose they are, yes. There you go.'

Lanning handed a cup to Patrick.

'Thanks, doc.'

Lanning offered Patrick a place on the three-seat sofa, under the window to the right of his desk. Patrick sat on the single chair Lanning had placed for himself to lead the session.

Jesus wept, is he attempting to begin, to hijack the session, Lanning thought. He sat behind his desk, feeling as if that reinstated his position as the man-in-charge.

'How have you been sleeping in general?' Lanning said, sipping his coffee and deliberately looking at the spine of a book on his desk. It was *The Body Keeps the Score*. That would have to be put into a drawer.

'Okay, I suppose. I think I got better sleep here, in the hospital. I got used to the bells and machine sounds, and being woken up in the middle of the night for blood pressure checks. It was nice to feel looked after all the time.'

Patrick smiled at Lanning and sipped his coffee. He seemed calm and thoughtful, but Lanning was concerned about Patrick referring to his time in the hospital as a fond memory. Most people, especially those who had suffered horrific injuries and loss, couldn't wait to get out of there, forget the horror, and were only too happy to be home again. There were always exceptions and *attachment* was something which could form a productive part of the shared therapy experience. It might be very interesting to discover any similarities and dissimilarities between Catherine and Patrick. PTSD was a ubiquitous initialism used these days, but the manifold points of psychological ingress and egress were fascinating. This start with Patrick could prove to be vital in potential outcomes. He would have to take his time to lay the groundwork. His experience had taught him how futile and unproductive it was to attempt to guide or cajole patients into any particular avenue of therapy. This would always be a marathon instead of a sprint.

'If you're ever struggling with particular issues between sessions, I would like you to feel you can always call me', Lanning said. He sat back and crossed his legs at the feet, wanting to give off the most relaxed version of himself: doctor as confidante.

'That's good to know, thanks. You said that already', Patrick replied. He half-smiled at Lanning and raised his eyebrows, as if he was pausing to let the psychiatrist respond.

Lanning sat forwards, trying not to rush himself, and trying to hurry a memory of making the twenty-four-seven offer before now. He couldn't summon anything. Jesus, was he truly becoming so forgetful of something so integral? He might have said *anything*. Was he so wrapped up in the possibility of renewed professional glory that he had begun to forget the bare essentials of the job?

'Of course and I meant it. I just want to reassure you that I'm as invested in this entire process as you are. It's important for you to feel complete trust and confidence in me. Ask me anything, anytime.'

Lanning sat back again but couldn't fake any more relaxation at this stage. Was Patrick trying to get under his skin, to challenge his commitment to this work? Perhaps that was a natural defence mechanism. Lanning upbraided himself for being so mentally fragile about such an innocuous statement, and so early on. He would need to work a lot harder on keeping his personal feelings in check, as hard as either of these two patients to find a place of greater strength in his psyche, possibly harder.

'How have you coped with any difficult emotions being back at home?' Lanning posed the question and immediately wondered about its validity and psychological merit. It was a broad and *flimsy* question with thousands of smaller questions built into it. What specific emotions did Lanning mean and when were they likely to appear; how did they relate to the things he and Patrick had talked about previously?

How did *anyone* cope with difficult emotions at home, and what were *difficult* emotions? He knew if he were asked the same question he might begin to mock or berate the nature of it and find himself taking pleasure in finding ways of questioning the question. How was he coping himself? Jane's death had been sudden. She had been killed in a car crash. She had called him on her way home to see how he felt about getting a takeaway that evening and been hit by a drunk driver while Lanning was considering the best option between fish and chips or a Chinese meal. Lanning had heard his wife's final words, her final sound, and the other sounds, the smash and crash of glass and metal, the concerned and shocked voices approaching her car, one of them calling an ambulance and the siren crying out as it arrived at the scene of her death. How did he cope with that afterwards? How did he cope as he walked slowly from his office, still listening

27

to his mobile phone, to get an idea of whether she was alive or dead. Listening as the sounds disappeared, as he arrived in Accident and Emergency, waiting for the ambulance to arrive, thinking to himself how perversely *lucky* it was that he was on-site already. That felt so twisted and wrong now.

Patrick didn't seem fazed by Lanning's question. He held his cup of coffee in one hand and used the other to gesticulate while he thought his answer through.

'That's an interesting question, doc. I thought I might want to get out of the house as soon as possible, you know, to put it on the market and stay in a hotel while it was being viewed and sold. But I didn't feel that way when I got home, not at all.'

Lanning felt relieved he hadn't been exposed as just another lazy psychiatrist, not yet. He nodded a couple of times.

'I couldn't wait for my sister to leave, after she dropped me back at the house. She was trying to mother me and all I wanted was to be alone. After she left, I walked around the house and found as many things of Maggie's as I could, that I knew she loved, collected them together and piled them into a metal bin in the back garden.'

Lanning had found himself continuing to nod, but stopped and refocused as soon as Patrick had said his last part before he sipped more coffee.

'Why a pile in a metal bin?' Lanning said. He sipped the last of his own coffee and eyed the pot, thinking he might need more immediately.

'I wanted to burn it all in one place.'

Patrick raised his cup in the air and took a drink.

Lanning wasn't sure how to respond. He raised his own cup and drank the few tepid drops from the bottom.

Has he popped a street drug pill and decided it might help him express more in the session? Lanning thought, feeling guilty for his own lack of empathy, his pedestrian reaction. But it was an unusual thing to do, burning a dead wife's most treasured items.

'Was there any particular reason you decided to set fire to those things?'

Patrick sat back, like a man without a care, happy to indulge the doctor's curiosity.

'Fire can be so cleansing. Do you know what I mean?'

Lanning sat back and nodded, unsure why he had decided to ask such a leading question. Wasn't there a deeper reach he could, and should, employ here. Catherine would be arriving soon and they shouldn't be seen to be discussing issues such as this without the shared component. Catherine might feel at a disadvantage and retreat before they had even started.

'I don't really associate fire with cleansing, more to do with heating and cooking, security and warmth. But it could be used to wipe things clean, I can see that, yes.' Lanning was finally happy with his choice of words. That choice was everything in this setting. 'I think we should stop there and, if you're comfortable with it, take up the ideas of dealing with emotions again with Catherine.'

'Sounds good to me', Patrick said. He took his mobile phone out of his jacket and read something. Lanning opened a small window next to his desk and looked at his wristwatch. Catherine was due in just over five minutes.

The five minutes turned into fifteen minutes late. Lanning was considering whether or not he should call Catherine, or perhaps her father. Patrick had visited the toilets and poured himself another cup of coffee. He seemed to be happy to wait, occasionally looking away from his mobile phone, at the office door then at Lanning.

Jesus wept, this is going to hell already, Lanning thought. He poured himself the last of the coffee then started to fret that Catherine would be desperate for a cup. He had a jar of instant decaffeinated in one of his drawers. Why hadn't she arrived? Was she waiting outside? He had checked for that a few minutes before. He checked again — there were three people waiting for other consultants but she wasn't one of them.

'Patrick, I'm not sure where Catherine is. I was wondering if you would mind waiting outside for a few minutes while I try to contact her?'

'No problem, doc. Give me a shout when you want me back in.'

'Thank you, Patrick. Hopefully we can sort something out as soon as possible.'

They only had an hour booked and a third of that time had already gone by. Lanning took some consolation from having spoken to Patrick, but the entire point of this time was to be *shared*.

9

Catherine looked at her cup of black coffee, getting colder by the second and too bitter to drink. She had finished the milk her father had bought and couldn't be bothered to buy any more. She tried to remember exactly how much, or little, sleep she had had the previous night. She guessed it was a bit less than two hours. That was a similar length to the night before that and most of the other nights since she had returned home. Nights in the hospital had been difficult, particularly in the last few days, dealing with another patient crying out the same phrase, *'Kevin, come and see me'*, but that had felt right, something expected, constant care on hand and an awareness of dealing with pain and suffering, one eye always open to the needs of the many. She had assumed her normal sleep pattern would return.

The quiet of her home was too much after the hospital. Even with the knowledge that Harry was dead, she had been able to talk to Lanning every day and imagine she might begin to feel like herself again when she could see and feel a sense of her life before the accident. But she felt as dead as her lover and as if she might always feel that way.

Catherine looked at the kitchen clock. The time looked wrong. She had glanced at her mobile phone before finally getting up and was fairly certain she remembered a different hour. She realised British Summer Time had begun the previous weekend. She began to think about what day of the week it was. Her father had visited her two days before and mentioned the weekend twice, so today must be Monday, or perhaps that was three days ago. It might be Tuesday. She had always been very careful about planning time, organising events, a work-life balance which suited her, and Harry. They had loved to wild camp, as often as they could. She would arrange to meet him back at the house after work, having packed their rucksacks the previous night, change as soon as they arrived home and be on the road as quickly as possible. Everything felt so rapid and well ordered; she had felt happy and free of burdens then, as if she had been destined to be with Harry, that he had always been the missing and perfect part of her life which had given her the energy to fully realise her ambitions. But he was gone now and she couldn't imagine organising anything, even shopping for food or toilet rolls. She only wanted to sit and stare at the framed Modigliani reproduction Harry had bought for her on their last anniversary, mounted over the fireplace in the lounge. Time could pass by now without order or care. The dust would build and she would transmogrify into a version of Miss Havisham.

Catherine woke up to the sound of her mobile phone buzzing and the sight of her coffee mug on the carpet below her hand and a half-moon of brown dribble around the mug's lip.

The display read: *Lanning*

She let the phone vibrate over and over until it stopped. There was another single buzz a few seconds later and *Voicemail (1 message)* appeared on the screen. She stared at the phone, half-expecting Lanning's voice to begin slowly telling her how disappointed he was she hadn't picked up and how he would like to find out how she was feeling. That could wait. He would still be curious when she decided to respond. His checklist would be ready whenever she was.

Catherine needed to use the toilet but felt heavy with fatigue and a numb sense that she still had a lot of the daytime to get through before she could tell her body it would be all right to sleep again. The needs of her body could wait as well. She knew Harry would cope better with the loss of her. He would have become very practical, grieving in short bursts and privately but getting on with the living: sorting out her pension payments, her life insurance, bank account and the rest. He would have contacted her family and friends, organised a memorial service and thought about how he could best honour her life and name. He would have looked after her in death as well as he had done in life. He wouldn't have allowed himself to fall into darkness and lie there staring into forever.

If she had been the one to die, he wouldn't be ignoring phone calls and daylight. Was she dishonouring his memory by being so indolent?

She had a shower, washed her hair and moisturised her face. She looked at her make-up bag, thought about how crazy with lust her bright red lipstick— *L'Oreal Paris Color Riche Satin* — had made Harry, and zipped the bag shut. She made her bed, their bed, and opened the bedroom curtains. They had separate wardrobes and she wasn't ready to look into his. She knew the scent of him would drop her to her knees. There was still a half-empty glass of cloudy water on Harry's bedside table and two strands of his hair on his pillow case. His DNA was everywhere. He wasn't anywhere to be seen or heard but he was still present.

Catherine plucked his hairs from the pillow, put them into a tissue and placed it into her jewellery case. She picked up his bedside water, sniffed it then drank it, holding the liquid on one side of her mouth, as if she was trying to keep the feeling of his tongue locking with hers.

She felt immediately repulsed by her behaviour. What would Harry say having watched her? He would probably be careful choosing his words, slowly asking her if she was feeling all right, whether or not she needed to lie down and rest. He had a look about him when he was feeling uncertain of something or someone; she would have seen that and known he had felt a drop-away of respect and love for her. She looked to her left, at the photograph on her bedside table — the two of them on the island of Poros, just over a year ago. They had just finished watching a film outdoors, on the roof of the local post office, a print of the original *The Pink Panther* film. Catherine remembered it from childhood and laughed all the way through. They both looked so happy in the image, so full of that moment on the Greek island, as if they would always be there, forever watching the sun set across the Saronic Gulf as Peter Sellers blundered through another scene in the film.

Catherine's phone began to vibrate on her dressing table. She stood up and looked at the front screen.

Lanning

She let it buzz to silent again, waited for a few seconds, chewing her bottom lip, feeling guilty, as if she had been caught in the act of negligence and was being judged in every movement and breath. She picked up the phone: *Voicemail (8 messages)*. Catherine looked at her bedside photograph again, at Harry's confident smile.

'I know I should. I know', she whispered to him. She pressed the voicemail number and waited for the automated response to finish, pressed one to retrieve the messages and kept looking into Harry's eyes.

10

Patrick was disappointed by having not met Catherine. He had woken up very early on the day of their first shared therapy session, excited to think he would finally be in the same room as the one person on the planet who knew what he did. He got out of bed quickly and used the bathroom, looking at his face in the mirror for the most amount of time since he had arrived home and deciding he needed to wash his hair, look the best he could manage. He still had three cuts healing around his cheeks and nose but he could still trim his beard and his sideburns and try to give a good first impression to Catherine. She deserved the most unique part of him, she had lost so much.

Patrick towel dried himself and applied a small amount of hair wax to his fringe. He needed to cut his hair but didn't have the time or focus today. He made his bed, rearranging his pillows. Even though Maggie was gone, he kept himself to his usual side of the mattress.

Should he wear a tie and jacket, iron a shirt? That might seem too formal and stuffy. It might inhibit the therapy and make Catherine imagine he wasn't friendly or approachable, the two things he remembered from interview technique classes in careers lessons at school. Patrick often thought of the advice his mother had given him when he was a nervous child, about to visit a friend's birthday party, 'Always ask people about what they enjoy doing and why. Everyone loves talking about themselves, whether it's boring or not'. She had said more, she always said too much, but he had remembered the main part as something worth knowing.

Patrick made himself a cup of black Earl Grey tea, changed his mind after one sip and made a half-cafetiere using some of the *special* coffee Maggie bought from the covered market. The coffee smelled better than it tasted. He sniffed the open packet, a waxed paper with red and green trimmed twine around the top and bottom, completely redundant to opening or closing the packet, and probably applied to make the buyer feel environmentally friendly; or perhaps that colour combination was only used at Christmas.

Maggie liked *things*, the shining of them was the important part, she sometimes tried to explain to Patrick. She enjoyed primary colours and exaggerated designs and retro-style. She placed little items, with no apparent use, never drink mats or ash trays, on the edge of shelves, such as plastic frogs wearing straw hats, smiling and holding a fishing rod, with its long, thin legs crossed.

'It's kitsch. Kitsch is cool', she would say to Patrick.

Patrick poured his coffee into the sink, washing away the brown drops from the edge of the stainless steel, folded the coffee packet, tied the twine, green around red, red up and over green, into a bow, then threw it into the bin, which he noted needed emptying. Kitsch wasn't cool to him. He pulled the bin bag out and began to walk along the edge of the dining room taking away anything that was supposed to be cool for the sake of it and pushing each one into the heaving bag.

'Kitsch is *not* cool', he whispered. 'Kitsch is criminally uncool.'

He walked past a black and white photo of Maggie, taken at their wedding. She was bright-eyed and inevitably drunk, pretending to suck her cheekbones in to look faux supermodel.

'You don't need to see all of this', Patrick said to the image, turning the frame down onto its face. He spent over an hour walking through the home they had bought four years before, watching home interior TV shows together and decorating with sponges and boutique paint to recreate the programme images, taking all individual traces of Maggie away and placing them into an overstuffed bin liner.

10

Patrick carried the bag out of the back door, picking up a large metal bin Maggie had bought for a decorative shrub and walked to the end of the small garden. He took her things out of the bin bag by the handful, a few food bits and teabags crept in amongst the kitsch. Patrick smiled at the wet and sticky mix. And then he set a fire to the contents of the bin. The fishing frog melted slowly, its legs remaining crossed, no leaping to safety for this version of kitsch. Its smile seemed like the last thing to blacken and distort.

Patrick showered slowly, using Maggie's shampoo, conditioner and mango shower gel, concerned he might smell of noxious smoke during the shared therapy. He sang a happy medley of Sinatra songs, replacing the lyrics he couldn't remember with bah-de-dahs and boom-de-dooms.

'You make me feel so young, you make me feel there are songs to be sung', Patrick sang at the top of his voice, realising he hadn't done that since he was a teenager, when he and Celia would sometimes resolve to become a pop star duet.

He walked back into his bedroom and looked at Maggie's make-up, perfume and jewellery on the dressing table she had chosen from a house clearance centre. She had covered the bases of the four drawers with rose design liner paper and ignored Patrick's comments about the wood being rotten and likely to collapse at any point from woodworm. He had tried to convince her to consider a replacement from the IKEA catalogue, but she usually smiled and replied that the table deserved to be there, in the same way they did. Patrick didn't have a clue what she meant by that. He picked up the wicker waste paper basket, moved Maggie's jewellery to a book shelf and ran the side of his hand across the chipped varnish top of the dressing table, guiding a hairbrush, the make-up, her perfume and a packet of make-up wipes into the bin. He used a roll of her winter socks to dust the top of the table then threw them into the bin. By the time he left for the shared therapy session, all of Maggie's drawers and the contents of her wardrobe would be tied up in black bin liners, ready to fill the varied charity donation bags which came through their letterbox every month. The drawer liner paper was ripped into eight equal parts and pushed into the kitchen recycling bin.

'Reuse, reduce, recycle', Patrick said, smiling as he tried to push his left foot into one of Maggie's high heels, failing by a few sizes then folding it into the final charity bag.

He adjusted his collar and looked at the kitchen clock. He hadn't thought about how much time he had left to wait until the shared therapy session began, only that it was on that morning; the arrival of that hour would mean the official beginning of his new life, the hospital he had recovered in would give him a form of rebirth too.

He looked at his mobile phone. Celia had sent him three texts in the night. The first wishing him good luck in the session, the second asking him if he was coping. He wasn't sure what she meant by that. He was recovering physically and had enough to eat and drink, and who could honestly or accurately say exactly how their mind was *coping* with any part of the past, present or future. He didn't want to tell her he was excited to meet Catherine. He knew she would think he was deluded and full of denied PTSD. It wasn't worth the trouble of explanation. She would see the difference in time and stop asking him such banal questions.

Her last text was full of attempts at morale boosting, reminding him how kind and strong and supportive he had always been with and for her, how she wanted to do more for him now, that he only had to ask her for any help he needed. Patrick couldn't help but feel cynical again, that Celia was using her advertising savvy to try to create emotional slogans for his gradual recovery — perhaps she had a whole campaign lined up and ready to go — ways of binding his psychological wounds and showing him the ease with which his path might be found.

10

He opened her WhatsApp conversation and sent a smiley face and thumbs-up emoji. He had seen something on Twitter saying the thumbs-up emoji was a polite way of ending a conversation. That seemed right.

He left the house not caring he would almost certainly have over an hour to sit and wait for the session to begin. Being back at the hospital was all he wanted for that day.

11

Lanning sat back slowly and considered the text message from Catherine. It was brief and to the point: I can't face things today. I'll be okay. I'll try and be there next week. C.

He thought of calling her again, asking her, although wanting to beg her, if she might still consider coming in, offering a shorter session later that day, a brief introduction to Patrick then separate sessions in the week. He knew it was more than likely her interest and confidence would fall away exponentially from this point. There was only a small amount of time before the best opportunity he had found in his entire career for a genuine psychological breakthrough, a publication of merit, might disappear completely and he would become the box-ticking drone again.

Lanning looked at the framed photograph he kept of Jane in the bottom drawer of his desk. He had decided, after her death, he shouldn't have it on display as it was too distracting to be reminded of her happiness and laughter, of the fact that was gone now, when he was trying to heal himself and help others to do the same thing. She would have understood.

Lanning hated using texts as a way of communicating with anyone, especially patients, but times had changed and communication in one way or another was the most important part of his job, that and trust.

He picked up his mobile phone and began to write, checking the predictive text hadn't changed any words, which had happened a couple of times, thankfully only with colleagues, who had laughed the errors off, but it was still embarrassing and, potentially, damaging.

Hi Catherine, I completely understand your concerns about today, it's going to be a slow and careful process at the most sensitive time. I would really like to think we can find a way to accommodate you and make you feel completely safe. May I call you tomorrow to discuss possible options? Dr L.

Lanning pressed send, even though he was uncertain how professional or successful signing off as *Dr L* might seem. To him, that looked as if he was trying to be the cool psychiatrist, akin to a plastic, celebrity tele-doc in the USA.

He lowered his head and listened to his breathing, aware of how desperate he might look to anyone walking in. Fortunately, just walking in, in this department, was highly unlikely.

Within a minute Catherine had replied.

Okay. Perhaps I could come and talk to you, just you for now, sometime this week, if you have time available? C.

Lanning looked at his office door. Patrick was still in the waiting area. He had been in the department for nearly two hours. Lanning felt a rush of guilt in realising he had been feeling compassion for Catherine and annoyance at Patrick, and only because Patrick had arrived early. But surely arriving so early was a cry for help? The poor man must be in so much pain, so lonely and desperate to share, to say how much he needed support. He had set fire to his dead wife's possessions. He was probably at a major point of crisis and now left waiting for something to happen, for his psychiatrist to open his heart and reach out.

At least Patrick was present and was ready to be helped.

Lanning clenched his hands into fists and mouthed two expletives. He closed his bottom drawer. He didn't want Jane to see him making such a mess of things. If he couldn't feel the immediate differences in these two patients and respond to any given situation, how on earth would he be able to conduct the sessions together, gather relevant data and be of any use at all?

He sent Catherine a reply: Hi Catherine, that sounds like a good idea. I'm free from 8 o'clock in the morning for the rest of the week. Are you able to come in on one of those days? Chris Lanning.

He pressed send and felt another pang of oddness about his signature. He had mentioned his first name to both Catherine and Patrick, to all of his patients, but usually he chose Christopher instead of Chris; only his family and Jane called him Chris. But most of the time he was called doctor. First Dr L now Chris, what next — The Lann Man?

Catherine replied: I can come in on Thursday. Is that all right with you? C.

Lanning tapped his phone, watching each letter rise on his touch, keeping an eye on the predictive text and feeling his heart race: Great. Thursday at 8. Thanks. Dr Lanning.

He was a doctor and he would sign and behave and be a doctor, a healer.

Lanning put his mobile phone on to silent mode and looked at his wrist watch. He had just over three quarters of an hour until he had to see another patient. That was time enough to talk to Patrick and get a sense of how he was feeling now he had had time to see what the world might be like without his wife in it.

Lanning stood up and sat down again. He reopened his bottom drawer and took out Jane's photograph.

'I still miss you, every day, every minute. I'm not sure I can do this. How can I help them when I can't really help myself?'

He looked at Jane's unmoving, forever smiling face, her blue eyes, and wanted to weep. He felt empty and lonely. Then he looked at his office door, at his coat hanging from the hook on the back of it. Patrick was a few feet away. It was all waiting for him, for all three of them. Salvation, together.

12

Catherine read Lanning's text messages over and over, as if she might have missed some vital code, some indication of what she was supposed to do between then and the moment she sat down to talk to him. But they were just simple, friendly and supportive messages, rearranging a meeting she had missed, had completely forgotten about.

How would she ever look Patrick Hawton in the eye. She had let him down already. Her sadness and loss were equally matched by shame, a deep feeling that she had no right to talk to anyone else who had survived that nightmare, their experience and loss might easily be so much worse than hers. Her mobile phone began to ring, it was her father calling.

'Hello love. How are you? How did your therapy session go? I hope you don't mind me calling to ask you. I've been thinking about you all morning, wondering whether I should call or pop over. Would you like me to pop over?'

Catherine wanted to see her father. They had always been able to talk things through. She trusted him more than anyone else, especially now that Harry was gone. But there was something too probable about seeing him, too painful to think of at this time. She knew she would begin attempting to explain herself to him, about how she was truly feeling, the hollowness inside that made her aware the constant beating of her heart was utterly pointless, a countdown to her drifting away someday soon, ending the life this lovely father had helped create. No parent wants to acknowledge their own child's desire to die.

'I'm okay, dad. Thanks. Tired from the session, though. I'm not really in the mood for chatting about it now. I feel all talked out, but thanks.' She had spoken the words feeling as if she was being fed them by an autocue, they were the cliché of a post-therapy fatigue, something her father might have been expecting and almost grateful to hear.

'Well okay, love. What about us having a walk and a coffee tomorrow?'

Catherine closed her eyes tightly and pinched the bridge of her nose. She wanted to whine like a child, shout out that she didn't know about having a walk or a cup of coffee, and she definitely didn't know about another tomorrow.

'Er, can I let you know later?' she said, feeling the dampness of tears between her eyelids, yellow flashes were building in the darkness. She was enjoying not being able to see anything, perhaps that might make living easier now, no visual reminders, the blank slate of blindness.

'Course you can. I'm free whenever you need me to be. Let me know if you want me to bring any shopping over. I could bring the dog too.'

Catherine told her father she would send him a text later, that she loved him and said goodbye. As she put her phone onto the table she felt two waves — guilt for leaving her father potentially concerned about her, his offer to visit was probably out of desperation to look after her, and she felt regret for not having attended the shared therapy session. She knew she needed it and she needed it to begin immediately.

Catherine called Lanning, who seemed stunned to receive her call, saying he was talking to Patrick. She arranged to go to the hospital. She got dressed, applied some make-up, tidied her hair, left the house, got into a taxi and arrived in Lanning's department within half an hour.

She sat in the waiting area and looked straight ahead. Lanning's door, clearly marked with his name in bold black letters, was to her left. She felt outside of herself, as if she was in stasis and her soul was pushing through her skin, wanting to be anywhere else. She wasn't sure whether she wanted to scream with anxiety or liberation. Her eyeballs felt hot and tight.

She opened her mobile phone on *photos* and looked at herself as a moving selfie. The immediacy of her resting face was shocking. She looked angry. She didn't feel that way, but her eyes and mouth seemed to be sending out a clear image of enmity.

She had focused on getting to the hospital as quickly as possible and had deliberately stared at her mobile phone, reading as much of nothing as she could in the taxi, anything to take her mind off the moment when she would have to sit with Lanning and Patrick Hawton.

How did Patrick feel? Would she call him Patrick? What else was there: Mister Hawton, Other Survivor?

Catherine knew he had been in the department for a while now. Had he already said everything he wanted to on that day? Who would want to repeat those feelings for a latecomer? Would she be the only one expressing herself? Would it be easier to talk in front of strangers?

She hadn't spoken to anyone about the crash, except basic information, questions and answers, in Lanning's hospital room chats. That had felt almost staged, as if she was taking her part in some sort of exercise to help the health system tick its boxes. She hadn't even touched the surface of how she truly felt. That was still under her skin, in her veins and poisoning her. It was building in its virulence and she had to drain it quickly. But how would that happen and when?

'Catherine.'

She looked up slowly and saw Lanning smiling at her. It took her a moment to completely focus on him. She had been daydreaming and thinking to the exclusion of her surroundings.

'Would you like to have a chat?' Lanning said. He looked over his shoulder. Catherine saw his office door was open. The room looked empty.

'Has Patrick gone home?' she asked.

'No. He's gone to the cafeteria, downstairs, to have a sandwich. He suggested it. I thought it would give you and I the opportunity to talk together for a while.'

Lanning twisted his neck slightly, as if he was urging her to follow him, but also looking like a man who expects rejection, waiting to be told to go away.

'Okay, that's a good idea. Patrick sounds very considerate, very nice.'

'He is, yes. Would you like to follow me?' Lanning turned his body sideways and shuffled slightly towards his office. Catherine stood up carefully, using the metal arm of her chair to support her. Her fatigue from rushing had made her feel heavy.

'Would you care for a hot drink?' Lanning said. He lifted a kettle from the top of a filing cabinet and held it up for her, as if it was the perfect question mark.

'A cup of coffee, please. A bit of milk, no sugar. Thanks.'

'Coming up', Lanning said. He smiled.

Catherine noticed a slight tremor in his hand as he put instant coffee into the cups. She hadn't thought of Lanning as a nervous person before now. He had seemed engaged and professional, if a little bit tired and beaten down, when she had been an inpatient. She was curious to know what was making him respond in this way. Had Patrick told him something harrowing? Had Lanning reached breaking point after years of absorbing other people's traumas? Wouldn't that be a natural response for anyone, he was only another human being. It must be an odd profession, helping patients rebuild their mental health while slowly endangering your own.

'There we go', Lanning said. He put Catherine's coffee on the edge of his desk. She leaned forward and took it by the side of the mug. It was scolding hot to her. She almost let go of it, but managed to use her other hand to grip the handle, clenching her fingers to the burning palm and rubbing the discomfort.

It felt good to be dealing with active pain, forgetting her numbness for a few minutes.

13

Patrick made the decision to leave the hospital rather than complying with Lanning's wishes. He had pretended to agree with the doctor's suggestion that he wait in the cafeteria, drinking coffee and staring into space, until Lanning texted him to return to meet Catherine. She had finally replied that she was willing and able to come in to talk and was on the way. Lanning had been animated and moving quickly to arrange the conditions for her.

But Patrick was already tired of waiting for things to change and begin again. He felt as if he had waited for positive shifts for most of his life, doing the right thing for those around him and taking what ever scraps of basic *okay* were left for himself. He didn't know Catherine, and Lanning hardly at all, but he knew he was done with being treated like second best. The sessions were for shared therapy, not prioritise one person over the other. He guessed Lanning had assumed his early attendance as being keen to enter the therapeutic process and his efficient answers as self-awareness and composure, but that was a false image, a hangover from the days before Maggie died. How would Lanning have responded if he had been sitting with his fresh coffee and decided to cover his face with the entire contents of the mug while screaming out he had deliberately caused the crash because he wanted both he and Maggie to die. That might have put a different perspective on the session, and made the psychiatrist, supposedly an expert in human reasoning and behaviours, think twice before sending him off to get more coffee in a cafeteria two floors down.

The one and only reason Patrick was in the hospital on this day was to meet Catherine, find out her story and how she was

13

still alive, who she was before and after, and to begin the long job of dealing with the realisation he was a *new person.*

As tempting as it was to stay and be recalled by Lanning, to see her face and attend the truncated session with Catherine, he had a point to make, his side of things to amplify.

Patrick walked towards the exit, he wasn't in a hurry and his phone hadn't beeped a message received from Lanning. He didn't want to use the lifts, the memories of being transported in his bed between various departments was still too fresh and the entire building felt so familiar, in one moment a comfort zone, in the next an overheated sense of suffocation, dangers and bad news behind every door.

He stopped at a newsagent stand near the main exit and couldn't decide what to buy. He didn't need anything and the thought of magazines, fizzy drinks or chocolate made him feel angry, distractions he had already spent too much attention on. There was work to be done.

Patrick heard his mobile phone receive Lanning's message. It might have been Celia checking on him, but he knew she would be at work, and only emergencies took her mind away from her campaigns. He felt powerful, finally in control, the one who could decide how they would proceed. He took his phone out. Lanning's message was on the screen: Ready when you are.

No apology for keeping him waiting. No emphatic words for him to complete the group. Just the equivalent of calling him like a dog that wants a walk.

Patrick didn't want to destroy the possibility of any future sessions but he wanted Catherine to become intrigued by him and to have Lanning taking him seriously, to make him show as much consideration as he had done for Catherine.

He sent Lanning a reply: I'm feeling too tired and conflicted to talk any more for now. I'll be at the session next week. Thanks. Pat.

49

Within seconds his phone began to vibrate. Lanning's name and number waiting for him to swipe the green telephone symbol on the screen. He swiped the red decline instead and switched his phone off. He hadn't done that in a while and it felt like another small part of his pure release.

Four days and nine further messages passed by before Patrick replied to Lanning. The psychiatrist's last voicemail had sounded quite desperate.

'Patrick. This is Doctor Lanning again. I need to confirm you are safe and well. Please contact me immediately, either by email, text or a direct call, at any time of the day or night. If I don't hear from you within the next twenty-four hours I will be required to contact your in case of emergency family member, your sister. I hope to talk to you very soon. Thanks.'

Patrick shook his head and smiled. He had pushed Lanning to exactly the place he wanted and now was the right time to draw things down.

He found the doctor's number, pressed the dial button and waited, humming Sinatra.

'Patrick?' Lanning sounded tense.

'Hi doc. How are you?'

'I'm ... I'm okay, thank you. More to the point, how are you?'

'I'm doing okay now, better. It's been a tough time, you know.'

'I can imagine, yes. Would you like to talk about things now? Or perhaps come to see me tomorrow?'

Patrick mouthed *It Happened in Monterey*, imagining Sinatra crooning at The Sands in the Sixties, probably focusing the song on a beautiful woman in the front row of that night's performance, thinking how it would be to have her later that evening.

'I think I would prefer to wait until the shared therapy session. Would that be all right with you, doc?'

13

Patrick looked at his reflection in the large mirror above the lounge fireplace, switched his call to speakerphone and pretended it was a microphone.

He could hear Lanning breathe out heavily and thought about asking the doctor if it was because he was relieved or even more anxious.

14

All of Lanning's fears relating to his true abilities as a psychiatrist seemed to converge in the days after the failure of the first shared therapy session.

'*Why* did I think this would work, that I was the one who would be able to carry this off? I'm a joke', he shouted, walking around his home study.

He spoke directly to a wall mounted, framed black and white photograph of Jane, taken when they first met, when they were so young and never even considered time. He had it enlarged a short time after her death. There were other enlarged prints, taken as images of moments, their love-filled history played out, throughout their years together, framed and mounted on all the walls of the house; smaller table mounted images too. He cleaned the glass on each frame every Sunday morning.

He wanted and needed to see her all the time. He always felt she could still hear him through the photographs. He had read about part of the soul being caught in any and every photographic image of each person.

He hadn't cleaned the house or changed his bedsheets since she had died, he wanted her to have a permanent space.

Her grave was somewhere he couldn't imagine visiting, it was only a marker to say she had lived. The body beneath the ground was absorbed back into the earth she had loved to work with in the garden.

The house was where she had truly lived and would always be a part of.

'Seriously, Janey am I so redundant now? Am I actually capable of seeing this through, of helping these people to heal?'

Lanning always waited for an answer he knew wouldn't come, and he hoped it would stay that way. As much as he wanted to see and speak to Jane again and was aware his shrine-like modifications in the house might be considered as odd by some colleagues, he was also conscious of keeping his own mind as coherent as possible. If Jane appeared to him one day, sat down in her favourite chair by a sunny, open French window and sipped freshly made coffee, answering his questions in her calm and thoughtful way, he might still have enough sanity and reason left to realise his time was up.

'Are they both so damaged they won't ever have it in them to meet each other? I felt as if I was the director of some absurdist drama the other day, moving between scenes of logic which disappeared as quickly as it had appeared, running in a circle, starting and ending with a complete lack of communication and understanding. I couldn't direct traffic right now.'

Lanning knew he was whining and was very grateful Jane wasn't there to hear him. She had always comforted him in moments such as these, but he had felt ashamed of himself afterwards, making a determined effort to get through the worst of times in the dignified way Jane seemed to manage, but knowing he would eventually trip and cry again.

Lanning made himself some lunch and poured two glasses of Jane's favourite wine, Chilean Merlot. He used the same glass, still unwashed, she had taken her last drink from. He said The Lord's Prayer at every meal, even though it meant nothing to him and he hadn't ever really known all the words — who could be bothered to remember whether it was forgiving trespasses against us or Him? But Jane was a Christian and it meant everything to her, so he mumbled about the hallowing of His name and the coming of His Kingdom.

What would he do next. Was it possible to press some sort of reset button on the idea of the shared therapy sessions? The first, most obvious, thing to do seemed to be to wipe away all assumptions he had built up about Catherine and Patrick after they left the hospital. The one on one sessions he had with them while they were in-patients was all over and he knew now he needed to treat them as if he hadn't ever met them. They were basic outlines in two files. He would have to plan for as many contingencies as possible — one or both of them not showing up to a session, or many sessions, creating the most relaxed space possible, probably not the hospital, and what to do if they didn't talk to each other or argued, fell out about some details of the night of the accident. Traumatic memories were intensely personal and notoriously inaccurate.

He ate his ham and lettuce sandwich and wondered where he would hold the sessions. He had a couple of professional friends who rented office space for private sessions away from their hospital offices. Perhaps he could temporarily sublet one of those?

But that was still an impersonal location. There had to be something which would show his absolute faith in both of these people, what he was investing in them and the therapy. Lanning looked at the framed photograph of Jane over the kitchen sink, a split second of her laughter caught during their holiday to Florence, eleven years before. She loved to travel, Italy was a favourite. But she loved her home more than anywhere else, her sanctuary as she called it. She would always want others to feel the same security and grace she did. She would have wanted to help Catherine and Patrick.

He would use this sanctuary to help them now.

Lanning sent texts to both of them suggesting the next session at his home. He more than half-expected at least one of them to refuse, probably both. But, amazingly, they accepted immediately. Perhaps they were relieved to be starting over, to be away from the sterility of the hospital or just curious to know more about who he was. The last possibility was self-absorption on his part and he would need to stop thinking in that way or risk ending up as he had done during and after the aborted first session.

14

Lanning reorganised his home study on the morning of the new first shared therapy session. He wanted a fresh start for all of them.

He understood he would need to move some things around and make an effort to tidy up the areas they would be using, basically the entire ground floor.

He vacuumed and polished, cleaned the downstairs bathroom and changed three framed photographs of Jane for original watercolours she had done as part of an evening art class. She had done lots of other classes, always keen to use her new skills immediately. Their Tuscany journey after six months of Italian had culminated with them deciding they would buy a villa there when Lanning retired. One of the watercolours depicted the villa that inspired them. He took a few minutes looking at it, wiping dust from the frame glass and knowing he would never visit Italy again or sell their house. The painting was as close to an idyll as he would ever be again.

He poured three heaped spoonfuls of ground coffee into a large cafetiere and filled the kettle. He became aware of the kitchen needing cleaning attention and set about the sideboards with antibacterial spray and the floor with a broom. He wiped the inside of the fridge too, then stopped and shook his head.

'I think that's enough, don't you?' he said aloud, imagining talking to Jane and her nodding approval.

Ten minutes until they were due to arrive. Was the house warm enough? The hospital was always too warm for him. Lighting the fire in his home study, where he was planning on holding the session, would take too long if he waited any longer, but if he started it now it might be ready for the majority of their shared time. The day was too warm for a fire. Lanning usually didn't feel the cold and had to ask Jane whether she would like the fires lit, windows opened or closed, always wondering whether or not he might be seeming self-centred for not paying more attention.

The first knock on his front door made him jump. He had been rehearsing his opening lines to Catherine and Patrick. They weren't scripted, although he had written some notes, but he wanted to present some thoughtful ideas to them and talk about the idea of freedom, safety and time available for both of them, that they should feel free to express themselves together or alone, that they weren't under any obligation to say anything until they felt they could. He was reminded of a Quaker meeting Jane had taken him to where the congregation sat in contemplation and remained silent until the spirit moved any one of them to offer something to everyone else. He had found the approach fascinating but not the content of the offerings. He knew Jane was happy he had made the effort. That was his offering.

The second knock made Lanning feel guilty and ridiculous, as if he had been caught masturbating.

He checked his hair and teeth in the hall mirror and opened the front door. Catherine and Patrick were standing side by side, both smiling at him. He hadn't felt as numb and terrified since Jane had been brought into the hospital after her accident.

'Please, do come in. I'm so glad to see you both here.'

Lanning was aware of how effusive he was being. Jane had told him, on more than one tense occasion, that he didn't need to overcompensate to draw people to him, that his intelligence, kindness and warmth would always be enough. He briefly looked at a small photograph of her, on top of a bookcase, and nodded a sorry.

'Would you like a drink, a coffee or tea, water?' Lanning said, leading them into his study. He had two sofas in the room, in an L-shape, and an armchair he had dragged in from the lounge. He had opened the curtains all the way, unusual these days, and opened the French windows on to the patio. The sun was covering the garden and there were many colours in the flowerbeds. He had made sure the grass was cut and light filled the study.

'Whiskey and soda for me, please', Patrick said. His face slowly grew into a grin. Catherine laughed. Lanning had believed Patrick's request for the whiskey and begun to think of a careful reply, not wanting to seem judgemental but not wanting alcohol or any other drug use in the sessions. He could have wept with relief when he realised Patrick was making a joke. 'Coffee is fine. Thanks, doc.'

'Same for me, please', Catherine said. She put her rucksack onto the floor next to the sofa end by the patio and sat down. The sun caught the side of her face and Lanning remembered how much Jane liked to sit in the same spot on summer mornings.

Lanning made the coffee, almost forgetting he had already filled the cafetiere. He listened to the building heat in the kettle, arranged three mugs on a tray with the milk and sugar and a plate with two kinds of biscuits. Catherine and Patrick were chatting and sounded as if they were having a nice time of it. Such a relief and such a surprise. Lanning wondered if this easy-going start might help or hinder the shift to talking about such incredibly deep and terrible memories and emotions. He knew that casual conversation was a potentially strong bonding exercise but also it might act as an inhibitor when truly attempting to open your heart. He wouldn't be able to talk to any of his casual acquaintances about his feelings after losing Jane. Any relatable fact they might have told him about their lives would always bring a subconscious comparison to mind and he would inevitably avoid laying his soul out for them to see. Its floppy decay would be repugnant.

He carried the tray through and poured the coffee, offered the biscuits then sat in his armchair. Catherine and Patrick sat quietly and waited for him to begin. Now he felt oppressively warm again.

15

Catherine didn't sleep at all the night before the shared therapy session at Lanning's home. She had accepted his idea of moving the location because he seemed so passionate about it, so insistent even though he was clearly attempting to put her at ease and create the impression it was the most productive way forward for all of them, and something did need to change after the debacle at the hospital. She guessed he had copied and pasted the same text to Patrick.

It sounded so simple but it made her feel even more anxious. The hospital had given her a sense of order and officialdom, a place where people are cared for and pass through, and there are lines between staff and patients. Everything was finite. But being in Lanning's home was going to be very different. She had passed the point of any curiosity about him, although that hadn't really been on her mind at all. She respected him for his profession, his obvious skills and experience as a person who could and would help her. Entering Lanning's space might mean she was confronted by something too personal and affecting, that it would be a catalyst of destruction in the process. It might be something relatively unimportant but enough to make her unwilling to return. She might see a book she hated or an uncleaned toilet. And what about the possibility of his wife or lover or child or anyone else being in the house at the same time as she and Patrick. She couldn't stand the thought of someone outside their group overhearing her or placing her in a state of paranoia, unable to express herself.

She was still working through her own idea that they might hold the sessions in each of their homes on a rota. The positivity in that might be a sense of atmosphere to provide a backdrop to any memory and a frame of reference when needed. The obvious negativity for both she and Patrick was the possible feeling of emotional invasion every three weeks and the virtual impossibility of ever getting away from the past. She decided she would talk to Patrick and Lanning about it during the session. Would she lose sleep the night before every session, would she lose more than just the one night before any sessions in her own home? She and Harry had enjoyed entertaining friends and family in their house but this process had nothing to do with leisure activities. This was about rebuilding her will to live. Was that truly something to try at home?

'Is this a good idea? Are you all right with me talking about what happened?' Catherine asked Harry.

'It's fine, Cath. It's necessary. You need someone to help you. This is too much to carry alone. Let them help. I'll be waiting for you. I promise I won't go anywhere. I couldn't leave you if I tried', Harry answered.

'But I don't even know them. I don't know if I can trust them. What do I say to them about what happened? Do I lie or tell them the truth? I love you and I want to keep that in my head and heart. I'm scared about what they might say if I'm too honest about what happened', Catherine whispered. She ran both of her hands through her hair and felt Harry kiss her forehead. He always knew how to comfort her and when to leave her to find her own way.

'It's going to be all right, Cath. Tell them whatever you need to, to feel better about living. You need to be alive. You're not ready to come and find me yet. You need this and nothing you say can change anything or hurt us.'

Catherine looked into the bathroom mirror and stared at her widening eyes; curiosity turning to surprise turning to fear.

She felt Harry's hands around her waist. She was warm and secure. She closed her eyes and turned around, waiting for him to embrace her, but he had left the room. She heard the bedroom door close and ran to see the street. A red car passed by. Harry was on his way.

Catherine made toast that stayed in the toaster and poured cereal that remained dry in a bowl. She settled on a large cup of coffee and stared at her dark reflection in the television screen.

The first part of the morning was grey and slow, the sunset fog making her view of the world outside seem as shutdown as her energy and hope. She kept looking at her mobile phone, checking the passing minutes and wondering if she would receive a text from Lanning cancelling the therapy session, telling her the whole idea had been a big mistake and he couldn't see her anymore, that she would be referred to another psychiatrist she hadn't previously met, who would treat her as a number on a file. She imagined receiving a first and last message from Patrick, telling her good luck and goodbye. Were they supposed to communicate outside of Lanning's supervision? What were the guidelines, were there any hard and fast rules about this sort of thing? She added to her list of questions, eight of them already. This was beginning to feel like a job, something she would have to manage. Her *real* job had given her all the time she might need after the crash, although her best work friend, Niamh, had begun to make noises about how much she was missed, making Catherine wonder if Niamh had been tasked, by their boss, to lure her back to the office sooner rather than later, or work from home. She knew her colleagues well enough to realise there wouldn't be any insensitivity involved, just an honest appraisal of the hole her absence left in their small team.

Catherine was wondering if she had time to make more coffee or perhaps a smoothie. Harry loved those, but she really didn't and should be leaving within the next five minutes, enough time to use the bathroom and get out of the front door. She had decided to walk to Lanning's house; Google had told her it was two miles away and her health app had reminded her how little exercise she had been taking recently.

The journey took her past an empty apartment complex, which looked in good repair but was covered in metallic security window covers. The grassy area in front of the buildings was freshly cut and two dustbin brick shacks were tidy. Catherine wondered where the residents had gone. She imagined a plague sweeping through, leaving no traces of those lives, just open doors into empty rooms. She walked down a narrow path, next to a railway line, under a bridge and on to another path, past geese and ducks.

The sun began to shine and a breeze lifted her hair slightly. There were narrowboats moving along the canal, cyclists and joggers out, looking dedicated and moving with the sort of purpose both she and Harry had shown so many times, when every moment of their lives together seemed to be working towards something very special, something indefinable but with enough motivation to feel as if they would know it when they arrived. Could she ever feel that way again. It all seemed so unlikely. If life really was so fragile and everything anyone ever did was so connected to the next moment and the next and the next, and all of that was entwined with the vast probability of disaster, then what was the point of even trying? Death was always the only certainty. And being left behind was the worst of it.

Catherine felt her mobile phone vibrating. She stopped and took it out of the coat pocket, expecting it to be Lanning, doubtless confirming her presumption that the session would be called off.

The display read: *Dad*.

'Hi dad, I can't really talk right now. I'm on my way to therapy', she said, feeling slightly annoyed at her father. He knew what day and time she was seeing Lanning and Patrick and must have guessed she would be en route. He had already sent her a text wishing good luck.

'Millie's been hit by a car ... she's dead', he said.

Catherine had begun to walk and talk, she stopped again. It took her a couple of seconds to remember who Millie was. Her father's dog, only a year old.

'Oh, dad. I'm so sorry. That's awful. Oh god. Are you hurt?'

'Thanks love. I'm fine. She ran after a cat, the silly thing. I'm so sorry to bother you. I wasn't sure what to do. I had to carry her home. She was so heavy, but wasn't bleeding. Some people offered to help me, but I didn't want them to touch her. I've got to dig a grave for her. I'm really sorry. I'll let you go to your therapy. I hope it goes well. I'll talk to you later.'

'Dad, I'll come over after I finish. I'll help you. Let me help. Okay? Dad, are you still there? Dad?'

She heard her father breathing.

'It's all right, my love. I can do it. I just need a minute to calm down. I can do it.'

'I'm coming over later, Dad. Wait for me. I'll be there in a while. Cover Millie over and have a strong cup of tea with some sugar. Don't start doing anything until I arrive. Okay?'

Her father breathed again. Catherine could hear him trying to cry quietly.

'Okay. Thank you, lovely. I'll see you in a while', he said, then put the phone down.

Catherine's pace quickened. She felt purposeful and needed. Her father had always helped and supported her. She was the one who could help and support him this time, hold him up as he had always held her. Harry would be proud of her.

Catherine knew Patrick as soon as she saw him approaching. He looked around the same age as her.

As they got closer he seemed to realise who she was too. His face shifted from calm, staring into space to squinting eye contact. She wondered whether he wore glasses but had assumed he wouldn't need them until he arrived at Lanning's

15

house. Catherine reached the top of the driveway first. She thought it might seem rude to walk to the front door without her therapy partner but didn't want to make an introduction in case it wasn't him. She opened her rucksack and took out a bottle of water, looked at her mobile phone — one message, a sad face emoji and kisses from her father. She felt guilty that she had almost forgotten about the dead dog. She sent her father two love hearts and two kisses.

'Hi, are you Catherine?' Patrick said.

Catherine felt a rush of anxiety and excitement, akin to meeting someone on a first date. That feeling was countered in her by an image of Harry and the sense she was cheating him.

'Patrick? Lovely to meet you. This is all a bit odd, isn't it.'

Catherine immediately regretted using the word *odd* about something as serious as trauma psychiatry.

'Deeply odd, but it's really good to meet you.'

They walked down the driveway next to each other.

'I think I saw the doc moving around behind a curtain', Patrick said. 'I wonder if he's forgotten we're coming. That would be embarrassing and awkward.'

Catherine laughed and Patrick smiled at her. She realised the last person she laughed with was Harry, on the morning of his death. Before she had time to wonder what that meant, Lanning had opened his front door to welcome them.

16

Patrick couldn't have predicted the way he would feel about Catherine by the end of the first session, but he knew everything had changed.

He woke at the time he had done for many years, seven sharp. Having done the same job week after week had programmed his morning body clock, reliable and boring. Any residual feeling of being able to lie-in when he was in hospital had disappeared. His mind, and now his body, were ready to return to planning for the future. He hadn't told his family he had resigned from his job the week after the crash, a one-line email had taken care of that and his boss had already sent through his P45 and paid a final salary into his bank.

Celia would be the last person he might tell. She would become didactic and moan on at him about the great value of work and routine, the enrichment of his life and skills. She would have begun sloganeering for the good of his soul, how he should *find himself and the right fit for him*. When she became too overbearing in her sense of order through easy sentences he wanted to scream at her. The right fit for him now was silence, keeping his thoughts ready for Catherine and Lanning. They knew the value of beginning something new and realising how to let go. Fate, whatever that might be, had pushed the three of them together and pushed away all the encumbrances of the past. Maggie wasn't here anymore. Her life seemed like part of a dream to him now. There were photographs of her alone and others where they had posed together for happiness and the creation of a memory which didn't reflect anything about the time it was taken. He had almost perfect recall of his thought process in the second each image was caught. Most of them were relating to wanting to be somewhere else with someone else. He hadn't hated his wife but she had always felt a major part of his indolence, settling for easy options and never pushing himself to go after the things he actually wanted, even if they had been impossible to have. He only had one life, that cliché was even more apt these days, and he wanted to restart it immediately. Catherine and Lanning were his arbiters of clarity. Patrick wasn't usually interested in clothes. He had bought a collection of outdoor shirts and trousers a few years before when Maggie had suggested they try regular wild camping, although that idea was quickly forgotten after a weekend of bad weather and arguments, culminating with Patrick being told to spend the last night sleeping in the car. That was when he had begun to plan his departure from her.

He wanted to look smart. Wearing a suit seemed too much. He only had one and he had worn that at Maggie's funeral. She had bought it for him as a wedding anniversary present. He didn't want or need it and the expense of it reminded him of all the gifts she had given him that were essentially useless to his life, such as the pen she had proudly bought him for his first birthday after they met. 'I thought this would help you on your way to becoming a full-time journalist', she had said. He smiled and kissed her, but wanted to remind her that journalists used laptops and their smartphones and a lot of other tools that didn't have any connection to a pen. He couldn't remember the last time he had used one, except a cheap *Biro* from the kitchen drawer to make up a quick shopping list.

He picked out a black and white checked shirt and a pair of khaki trousers. He wore a t-shirt under the checked shirt and put his tweed jacket on over the top. He pulled out his dust-covered tan desert boots from the back of his wardrobe to finish the therapy outfit and realised he hadn't worn either the jacket or the boots for a long time because Maggie had called them ugly.

Patrick had time to kill before he left for the therapy session. He re-read a good luck message from Celia then deleted it. She had typed more emojis than letters and he thought it was rushed and insincere. What was the point of sending it? He had worked with someone, for years, who only wrote *Best Wishes, Ian* in any and every office card, regardless of the occasion. Celia used words for a living but seemed incapable of discerning the value of them if it didn't equate to a product launch and its potential impact and imminent market position. She seemed to have forgotten to use her heart with her head.

Patrick knew he had to reply to her, otherwise she would call and visit him. He wrote a Thanks and added a heart emoji for maximum reassurance, unable to bring himself to type Love You, and looked again at Lanning's last message, confirming the agreed session time and address. He had already made the walk to Lanning's front door, more than once, having made sure the doctor was at the hospital. He had pressed his face against the downstairs windows and taken photographs of the rooms he could see, the many wall-mounted images of the woman he assumed was Lanning's wife. But where was she? The images seemed like an obsession, an exhibition of love and longing for the doctor and that made Patrick feel intrigued and slightly uneasy about who this psychiatrist really was. Might Lanning be an imposter, someone who needed a lot more mental help than either him or Catherine, perhaps a former patient who had never left the hospital and wandered the halls pretending to be a psychological health specialist, using empty office space and, having decided things were becoming too risky in the psychiatric unit, had moved the session venue to his home?

Patrick felt pure excitement at the thought of finally getting inside the house and meeting Catherine, as if there were many secrets waiting for him and ways of living he hadn't previously imagined possible.

What would Catherine look like in person? The idea of meeting her had become almost too much to think of anymore. Would he find her physically attractive? Would she see him in that way? Did any of that matter? Of course not. He was single again but thoughts about any future types of new relationships had quickly come to feel akin to threats.

He had to leave now. He knew how long the journey would take and he didn't want to be early or late.

He focused his breathing and looked at the trees and buildings, avoiding any eye contact with passers-by. He didn't want any details of those around him in his head before the session, keeping a blank slate upon which to begin his life again.

As he walked along the pavement, knowing he would soon see Lanning's two chimney stacks, he caught sight of a young woman walking towards him, she was the only other person on the street. He knew it was Catherine, it had to be. His stomach dropped and his legs felt as if they might just decide they were unable and unwilling to go any further.

'Hi, are you Catherine?' he said.

Of course you are, he thought.

17

Lanning felt confusion and panic after the first therapy session. He didn't know whether he would be able to go through, potentially, the same thing again next week. He had thought about the possibility of mutual trauma and made connections between the feelings Catherine and Patrick might share but hadn't included his own experiences after losing Jane. The session seemed to tear part of his soul open, or perhaps reopen the wound he had lived with since his wife had died.

'Is it wrong that I don't really miss her yet?' Patrick had said, downing the last of his third cup of coffee. He looked at Catherine, who hadn't said much in the previous ten minutes; she had nodded then shaken her head as if she wasn't certain how to answer such a difficult question and had taken the middle road of unsure but going along with what Patrick appeared to be saying. Lanning mirrored her response, following his training of wanting to move the session forward, allowing the freedom to express and not appearing judgemental, even though he was feeling outraged by Patrick's cavalier attitude. Of course he should be missing his wife, that was part of the grieving process. She had been a huge part of his life and had died in a sudden and horrible way. She was very young and must have left her family in emotional tatters. And here he was, her husband, asking them, a widow and widower of other car crashes, whether it was wrong he didn't miss her. It *was* wrong.

But Lanning knew he was feeling a surge in his own grief and this session, this moment and the feelings on display weren't about him and how he missed Jane. Catherine and Patrick didn't even know she had existed. They hadn't asked about a significant other in his life and probably wouldn't. Their assumptions might be that any partner had been asked to leave the house during the session time, wait upstairs or had divorced him some time ago. Curiosity was natural, but they had enough to deal with.

'It isn't wrong, no. I don't think there are any wrong emotions or thoughts after such a big change in anyone's life. Our minds act as a processing filter and quite often delay certain parts of healing because too much, too soon would be unbearable. It's different for each person and everything is valid and okay.'

Lanning took a few seconds of the following silence to think over what he had just said, quickly reviewing his own validity and wondering whether or not he was merely talking psychobabble to warm himself up.

Catherine and Patrick were both nodding in acknowledgement but he knew they might be beginning to rethink this therapy or wondering how long was left of the session, or perhaps what they might have for supper that evening.

'Do you miss your partner?' Patrick asked Catherine. She looked surprised and uncomfortable. Lanning was momentarily overcome with a desire to leap across his study and punch Patrick in the face.

What the hell was he trying to pull? Catherine was shaking her head slowly as if she couldn't completely understand his question but enough of it to be appalled beyond words.

Lanning was caught between wanting to rush to her defence, speak for her feelings, as he perceived them, and be the all-understanding voice of empathy and reason, telling them that everything was all right to talk about and to feel. He wondered whether he would be as protective as this if Catherine had asked Patrick the same question. Was his chivalry an act of inconsideration in itself, a sexist gesture?

'Yes, I do miss him, I miss him so much, every day, in ways that wouldn't have seemed feasible before the accident happened. And that's the oddest part of all of it, the fact that I feel as if so much more than his life ended on that day, as if whole sections of reality and normality disappeared and now I'm left with wondering if anything was true before it all happened. Thank you for asking that, Patrick. No one has been that direct and allowed me to feel as awful as I actually do. It's such a relief to be saying this out loud and not just in my head. It's too easy to imagine I'm alone in all of this and will be forever.'

Lanning was shocked. He would have preferred a more psychologically precise term, but shocked covered his initial response. He looked at his virtually empty writing pad, at his hands and at the place on the wall opposite where a vivid colour portrait of Jane had still been hanging the night before, at the sofa where Catherine sat now, remembering he and Jane making love on it when they moved into the house. Then he realised Catherine and Patrick were looking at him, clearly waiting for a way to move on in the session. That was his role, not the Knight, not the Defender. He was the Guide.

'Yes, thank you, Patrick. And thank you, Catherine. That was an extraordinarily honest answer. Beautifully articulated. Would you care to elaborate on the ways you miss Harry?'

Lanning wasn't sure about using Harry's name. He usually allowed trauma patients to set the pace; he would avoid certain terms, dates and names until they began to use them, but he thought this was possibly a breakthrough moment, and so early in the session work, and it felt right. If Catherine declined to use Harry's name from this moment, he would too. His confidence was increasing.

Lanning talked about the session to Jane later that day. He had always used their conversations, Jane's compassion, faith and insights, to decompress after hard days and missteps. Her belief in people, kindness and empathy was always a blessing and a curse for him — a constant reminder of how lucky he was to have her in his life and a source of depression for his own sense of lacking.

Since her death he had carried on that way, talking to a photograph he had taken of her when she had been caught unawares, turning around and spontaneously smiling at him in the most loving way, a look that still made him want to scream and cry and smash the house into pieces on the worst days with the hurt and loss that was constantly on fire inside him, but Jane would have despaired seeing him that way. She would have told him her death was part of God's Plan and he should go on, use his skills and experience, and even the pain, to help other people. But if she had been right and it was all part of some celestial plan, then the planner was a sadist.

'They both seem to be opening up and connecting well. Catherine seems to be more emotionally honest and Patrick seems to be willing to face the truth about his future without his wife. I can relate to that, although, I know, I'm not supposed to be relating directly to what they've been through. But I do believe I can help them more, potentially, by challenging myself to be more honest about what happened after you ... about now. What do you think?'

Lanning looked at Jane's photograph then closed his eyes. She would have taken a few moments, nodded a couple of times with recognition. She knew how much he valued her opinion and guidance, and she would have told him she understood what he was saying, but she was concerned he was possibly making a mistake by folding-in his own trauma into the shared therapy, even if inadvertently for the most part, especially as neither Catherine or Patrick had any knowledge of what he had been through, was still going through. That he had seen Jane's heavily wounded, dead body arrive at the hospital, watched the doctors and nurses working on her efficiently, even though all was lost, and understood the through-the-glass silent gestures which meant they were agreeing they had tried all life-saving procedures and the patient had died anyway.

He hadn't recognised her on that day. The body didn't look like Jane, just another patient come and gone. He had seen lots of corpses. Everyone who had tried to help her had nodded condolence at him and walked away to help the next person. He had watched her from a distance, waiting for the smallest sign of life still showing, a slight shift of her limbs or head, something to allow him to open his mouth and let the build-up of anguished sounds be released.

He couldn't move his legs towards her. He knew she would still be warm, the light blue ambulance blanket was pulled up to her chin. She disliked the cold but liked light blue things.

She often called death the long rest. He joked she had forgotten the title of the most famous of Raymond Chandler's novels.

His so-called skills and experience didn't mean anything there and then. Nothing he could ever offer would make her wake up again. He wanted to have a long rest too.

18

Catherine had Patrick's mobile telephone number now and she wanted to call him but felt as if she would be cheating on Harry. They had exchanged details after the session, as they reached the top of Lanning's driveway. Patrick had asked her if she would be interested in swapping numbers and her natural inclination as a people-pleaser had kicked in.

'If you want to talk or text, let me know', he had said, offering her his hand. She nodded and smiled and shook his hand but felt a sadness at the thought of not seeing him for another week. She thought about suggesting they find somewhere to have a drink, maybe some lunch, and keep talking but that might look pushy and awkward and breach the, still unspoken, rules of the session work. And she remembered she hadn't contacted her poor father yet. He was probably looking out of his kitchen window at the cover he had put on his dead dog. Death and its consequences were everywhere, all of the time and yet it seemed denied and hidden until the truth of it was brought home again and again.

Patrick had been very different to her pre-session imagined version. The only way she had been able to think of him was the sobbing, pale widower. She didn't have any reason for such an extreme presumption and, as she walked towards her father's house, she wondered whether she had wanted to think of him in that way to make herself feel better about her own way of dealing with the grief, that she was coping so much better than she had thought, always the strong and organised one.

Patrick was a good-looking and confident man, well-dressed, a bit older than her, and not Harry. Being in a relationship had always made Catherine feel oblivious to any other attractions. She could still acknowledge when men were funny or nice to look at or made an interesting point, but true attraction was a thing of the past, and that suited her. She had always wanted security and love, and Harry had given that to her.

When Patrick said he didn't particularly miss his wife that much yet, Catherine had been appalled by him. She had wanted to shout at him and tell him he was evil. But as he described his sense of things since the crash, she had begun to realise she was feeling and thinking in a lot of the same ways. Perhaps his honesty had served to expose her lies; if not lies then memories which had become rose-tinted in remembrance.

Catherine spent the afternoon helping her father bury Millie, collecting all of her favourite things: an old green and white quilted blanket, two soggy, orange tennis balls she liked to carry around, a ragged chew-toy duck called Ducky, which made a very annoying honk. Millie always managed to find the honk quickly, being told what a clever dog she was each day. Her collar and lead were added to the burial pile.

Catherine's father had already dug a hole at the end of the long and narrow family home garden. The garden was in two parts, separated by a trellis fence and a high and wide rose bush. The furthest end of the *secret* garden, as Catherine had grown up calling it, fuelled by her love of the Frances Hodgson Burnett book, was a small orchard. Millie was laid to rest among the apple trees. Catherine's father said the Lord's Prayer after patting the soil flat and they both stood in silence.

Catherine hadn't expected to cry. She had been through so much grief and pain and was only just beginning to process everything now. But as she thought about Millie's happiness and innocence and trust being wiped out in a heartbeat, she felt her eyes dampen and become blurred. She used her sleeve to wipe them dry and put her arm around her father's shoulder.

'Thanks love. It's so kind of you to help me with this, especially after everything you've been through. How are you doing ... with the therapy? Sorry, I probably shouldn't be asking that.'

Catherine kissed her father's cheek, a few missed bristles tickled the end of her nose. His aftershave reminded her of childhood and feeling protected.

'I'm all right. It was ... interesting, a lot to think about, but the doctor and ... other patient are very supportive and I think it might be good for me.'

Her father had always been tactful and careful about how much he should ask his children about their private lives. He hugged Catherine and they walked back to the kitchen. Catherine put the kettle on and made them both a cup of strong tea. Her father brought a box of cream horns from the fridge. They smiled at each other, ate and drank, and listened to Clair de Lune.

'She loved running between those trees, biting the fallen apples, rolling in the snow there', Catherine's father whispered. She knew he wasn't talking to her but nodded anyway. She looked down the garden and thought about Millie, about taking Harry to see the orchard for the first time, and she thought about Patrick, about texting him later, telling him about her day, about her loss.

She didn't stay with her father for supper, her mother would be there and Catherine struggled with the two of them together, making a fuss of her, insisting she stay with them for a while, that it might be a good idea for her to think about selling her house and making a fresh start. She wanted time alone. Time to consider contacting Patrick. How was he today? Had he thought about contacting her after the session?

Had he noticed the photographs of a woman in Lanning's kitchen? She had seen a small stack of them on her way to use the bathroom as they were getting ready to leave.

Catherine hadn't had time to study each portrait but the woman looked as if Lanning had known her for many years and the images were intimate enough for her to guess they were very close. Was he divorced? Had she left him? He was

75

an empathetic person but that was his job. Catherine couldn't imagine Lanning as a romantic.

She picked up and put down her mobile phone time after time that evening. How would she even begin a text to Patrick: *Hi Patrick, lovely to meet you...*

She didn't want to risk making a mistake about his good intention, giving her his number, and seem like an oddball who might contact him day and night with broad summaries about her thoughts and feelings. He had so much to work on too and she had to respect the unspoken trust that came with being allowed a direct line to him. She didn't want to call any of her friends, and definitely not Lanning.

She would wait until the next session, see how she felt after that and make a decision about extending contact with Patrick.

Catherine tried to focus her mind on something other than the therapy. She picked up a novel she had started a month ago, but she couldn't be bothered with the life of the main character, who seemed self-obsessed to the point of being crushed by his ego. She wondered if a Netflix Top Ten show might engage her, but the three trailers she watched were either unfunny, depressing or full of action and no intelligence, or all three.

She sent a text to Niamh, asking her if she would like to meet for a cup of coffee and a chat. Niamh, always reliable, replied within five minutes, saying she would love to.

Catherine went to bed and wondered what she would say to Niamh about Patrick that wouldn't make her blanch at the thought of beginning again, too soon, after Harry.

19

Patrick waited for the sun to rise. He looked at his reflection in the sash window that looked out on to the street and thought about how he might live the rest of his life, watching the harried morning faces walk on by.

He had two unread texts from Celia and had hoped he might receive one from Catherine. She had kept him awake last night, and was always in his thoughts these days.

The sessions had been running for a little over a month and Patrick was desperate for the progress he had decided for himself and Catherine to begin.

After the first shared therapy session, Patrick had wondered whether he would bother with returning the following week. He felt out of place and angry he hadn't expressed himself properly. Catherine must have thought of him as an ignorant slob, someone without the ability to have learned about the value of life, an insensitive fool.

He had said he didn't miss Maggie very much and watched both Catherine and Lanning's face switch from interest in his thoughts to shock and flickers of disappointment and momentary horror. And then he had followed up by asking Catherine whether she missed her partner. It sounded so flippant and tactless and hadn't come close to the point in his head. He had been trying to touch upon the ways he was coping, ways he might offer to Catherine, to help her. He had wanted to show empathy and support, for the correlation in their lives and what was left to be a foundation on which to rebuild themselves.

He had wanted Lanning to grab the point, immediately understand his thinking and apply his skills, broadening the concept and drive it on.

But it had all fallen on its face. The other two had been kind to him, left the ignominy hanging in the corner of the room and worked away from it with careful responses. Catherine had even shown him the kindness of pretending to relate to what he had said and thanked him for his insight.

Thanked for undiluted stupidity. Jesus wept. They should have asked him to leave.

The following session had been akin to starting again. He felt inhibited and didn't offer a lot. Lanning had done most of the talking. Catherine had asked questions about protocols, such as contact outside the sessions, privacy in Lanning's note taking and the potential limits to what they might offer in terms of intimacy, recollection and recriminations. Patrick wondered if the last question was a dig at his faux pas. He deserved it. But he believed in who Catherine seemed to be. He liked her, a lot, and wanted to talk to her more and often, feeling relieved when Lanning said it was up to the two of them if they made contact outside the session. They were adults and shouldn't feel confined by a once-a-week maximum limit of expression in the sessions. He had added they may need to talk about their own limits. Lanning would be available to them whenever they needed him.

Patrick sent Catherine a text that same evening and they met for coffee the next morning, at the place he and Maggie often visited for weekend jazz-brunches, which Patrick loathed and guessed Maggie only pretended to enjoy because her friends had recommended them as *'super cool'*.

'This is a nice place, have you been here before?' Catherine asked as she sipped her coffee.

'I used to come here with Maggie, but it always seemed like a chore.'

Patrick looked at the walls, covered in Hollywood retro posters — Monroe in *The Seven Year Itch*, Dean in *Rebel Without a Cause*...

'Why was it a chore?'

Catherine waited for an answer. She smiled and looked into Patrick's eyes. He held his breath before he answered. He had talked to Lanning, in private, about a method he might employ when he thought he was going to say something blunt, unformed and, potentially, upsetting in front of Catherine. His immediate response was that virtually every moment with Maggie had been a chore, that she was an impossible person, that they had a good sex life, but the rest of the time they were either arguing or not communicating, that they shouldn't have married and he had often imagined her gone forever — no relationship counselling, trial separation, divorce and division of property and assets. Just gone.

Holding his breath and counting to five seemed to dilute such extreme replies and allow him to couch his words in softer terms. He knew he would have to allow the truth about his life with Maggie out eventually, there was so much he needed to talk through, but he wasn't ready yet.

'They always seemed to play music I didn't like, and the coffee was always tepid.'

Patrick dropped his mouth into a sad clown expression and Catherine laughed. Her laughter had become his favourite thing. It was still a rare sight and all the more special for that.

'Did Maggie like it here? If you don't mind me asking', Catherine said, sipping her coffee, smiling, pointing to her mug and giving Patrick a thumbs-up. She still made sure her questions relating to Maggie were within the limits they had talked about some weeks before. Patrick didn't ask about Harry very often. He had felt jealousy over Catherine's dead lover almost from the first moment they had begun talking outside Lanning's session. He wanted Catherine's attention and concern, but he was careful to seemed fully engaged and interested when she did open her heart to his loss. The dead had taken their turn and used the time they were given.

'She did. She used to suggest we come to jazz-brunches on Sunday mornings.'

'Did you?'

'Unfortunately yes. Can you imagine giving up croissant, coffee and reading the paper in bed for listening to badly improvised ten-minute trumpet solos?'

Catherine began to laugh again. She put her coffee on the table and leaned forward. Patrick wondered if he had mistaken upset for amusement, but she was definitely laughing harder than before.

She took a few seconds to regain her composure.

'Oh, god, you make me laugh so much. Thank you for that. My dad used to play jazz all the time. We hated it, my mum in particular. I had a flashback of him pretending a baguette was a saxophone, the end of it falling on to the kitchen floor and our dog eating it.'

Patrick waited until they were leaving the cafe before making the suggestion he had been thinking of for some days.

'Can I ask you a personal question?'

Catherine stopped and looked at Patrick as if she was expecting to laugh again.

'Of course. Isn't that what all of this is about, the personal questions and answers?'

'Absolutely. It is, it really is. But this isn't about how we feel after what happened. This is about how we could have felt, still could feel.'

Catherine nodded twice and put her hands in her pockets. Patrick wasn't sure whether she was cold or using negative body language. Perhaps hands in pockets were just that. He was annoyed he had become so analytical since beginning the shared therapy.

'Okay, this sounds big. Ask away,' Catherine said. She pulled out a tissue and blew her nose, keeping both hands out of her pockets.

19

'We seem to have a connection ... we do have a connection now. I think we've become friends. There were always things I didn't say or do with Maggie, different ambitions to go to various places, have a proper go at living. I feel strangely free of those constraints now. I was wondering how you feel?'

As soon as Patrick had said the final sentence he knew he had made a mistake with the timing and delivery. He had put forward exactly how he felt but articulated it in a way he understood made very little sense, and might be interpreted in multiple ways. One of those ways could be as a sexual hint between he and Catherine.

Added to that, he hadn't held his breath at all, taken the requisite seconds to think things through, and had talked as if he would find it easy to move on from his wife's death, that she had been ruining his life anyway and he had somehow found new choice and opportunity with Catherine. He wanted to begin to undo the damage but could see a look in her face which seemed to be looking for a way to leave.

'Sorry, that was utterly incomprehensible. I was trying to say something about healing and getting on with life, the best ways to do all of that. It came out as rubbish.'

Catherine seemed to relax.

'It's fine. I understand. I think we should talk about all of that with Lanning, don't you?'

'Yeah, that sounds good. I'll see you at his house tomorrow.'

'See you there.'

Catherine leaned in to Patrick and kissed his cheek. She hadn't done that before. It felt incredible.

As he walked home he wondered if she *had* actually understood what he meant. Perhaps it had scared her to think of letting go of Harry in some unexpected way, and taking *his* hand towards a new life, feeling something similar to him. Perhaps she had felt a shift and was considering going with him.

What would Lanning have to say about that?

'This wasn't what I thought it would be, Jane. I'm feeling as if they just come here out of obligation, as if I'm not really helping them at all.'

20

Lanning sat in his underwear on the bed he had shared with Jane while they were married but not after her death, deciding to live mostly downstairs, sleeping on the sofa in his home study. He had almost forgotten to move his bedclothes before one of the sessions, throwing them behind the sofa seconds before Catherine and Patrick entered the room.

He wore a t-shirt, boxer shorts and socks, his hair still damp from the shower. He had filled the abandoned bedroom with the photographs of Jane removed from the ground floor for the session work. He could see her face everywhere in this room. The morning sunlight showed dust motes, like signs of life itself, moving across her eyes and smiles.

'You're helping them by just being there', he heard Jane's voice say, looking around the room for any change of expression.

Lanning moved to Jane's side of the bed and slowly laid his head near her pillow, although he always took care to not actually touch it. There was still a slight indent where she had slept through her last night on earth. She had been an easy sleeper. She would say goodnight to him, kiss his cheek, switch her light off and he would know she was asleep within minutes.

They hadn't been able to have children. Jane had been diagnosed with PCOS and had decided she wanted to use her degree in Art History and dedicate herself to studying the works of Da Vinci. They had talked about adoption but never taken it any further. Whenever Lanning had begun to wonder whether they had missed out on something, he consoled himself with a list of pros and cons. The top pro was always: *not having to endure sleepless nights with a baby...*

Now that Jane was gone he was enduring more sleeplessness than he would have imagined possible. At least the sleepless nights with a baby would have ended, the baby would have grown up and he wouldn't be so lonely all of the time. He had a brother, who had lived abroad for years, but they hadn't contacted each other since their parents had died. Jane's family had always been aloof with him. He still received a Christmas card from her sister but he hadn't spoken to any of them since Jane's funeral.

The house was all he had left. This was where they had lived and loved, and this was where he was helping Catherine and Patrick to begin again. That was what he would live with and for. Jane would approve of that.

'They seem to be getting along very well. I find myself wondering whether I should ask them what sort of things they discuss when they meet each other outside the weekly sessions. What do you think?'

Lanning sat up, feeling light-headed. He looked at a different photograph of Jane and waited.

'No, no. Don't do that. They're helping each other and looking to you for support and guidance. Asking them questions about their private conversations would be a bad mistake.'

Lanning nodded, then looked at Jane again.

'But what if they're taking the wrong turns? Shouldn't I be monitoring where they're heading?'

'You know that doesn't really mean anything. That's psychobabble. You only need to be there for them. The way you were always there for me, my love.'

Jane's voice sounded so clear in his head. He wondered when he would forget what she had sounded like, when the voice would be his impersonation of her. Was that already happening? Did he have any recordings of her?

Lanning drank too much coffee before Catherine and Patrick arrived for the next session. He had convinced himself his thoughts and insights would be so much sharper with additional caffeine in his bloodstream. But it hadn't worked in the past and

20

all it served now was an increase in his performance anxiety and sense of self-deluding fakery. Had he truly helped these two people or were they helping themselves while he tinkered with the outcomes?

Facilitator suddenly seemed like his least favourite word in the English language.

'Come on in. How are you?'

He tried to look and sound as jolly as he could — Good Old Santa Lanning — but thought he sounded plain odd. His face seemed fixed in a smile which hurt the corners of his mouth, but he didn't seem able to let it go away.

He made more coffee, Camomile tea for himself, and biscuits and glanced at his mobile phone lock screen photograph of Jane, taken when they visited Chamonix for skiing. Jane had always talked about going but Lanning had avoided the subject, nodding in agreement and not taking it any further. His brother was a ski fan, along with extreme sports, and it had always seemed to him *the* recipe for disaster, something that might look like adventure at the beginning of a James Bond film but would, almost inevitably, get them broken limbs, knocked out cold or accidentally leaping off a cliff into an abyss. He had enjoyed the holiday in spite of himself. He wished he had taken more time to listen to the reasons behind Jane's thoughts and passions. Had he only been a superficial husband and lover — someone who took care of the basics of married life but only ever aimed for *minimal effort required*? It was too late to change anything but regret was difficult to get away from.

'Here we are.'

Lanning walked into his study and put the coffee and biscuit tray on the large reading table he had moved in from the unused lounge. They had all moved their chair placements over the weeks and now they sat in a spaced circle, like a debating team organising lines of enquiry.

'How have you both coped this week?' Lanning said, deliberately avoiding eye contact after the question, reaching forward to collect his coffee and pick up two Garibaldis.

'Good, really good', Catherine began. She picked up her coffee but no biscuits. Lanning had added three gingerbread men to the plate after hearing Catherine and Patrick talk about them the previous week. Perhaps they thought he was attempting to trick or test them in some way. But he was only trying to get closer to them. Both approaches felt suddenly very wrong. A gingerbread man was really just a biscuit but in a psychiatric setting it was also a statement of sorts. He vowed to stick to plain digestives in future. 'I got stuck into some gardening I've been planning and finally cut the grass. That took me hours', Catherine said. She seemed happy and relaxed, fully at ease for the first time. Lanning smiled at her and nodded, remaining silent. He looked at Patrick, who was sipping his drink and holding one of the gingerbread men. The head was already missing.

Did that say anything about his character, that he had decided to decapitate the treat at the beginning of its consumption?

'I've been working on something for my sister', Patrick said. He had finished eating the second gingerbread arm. Lanning was beginning to wonder if Patrick was subconsciously devouring the biscuit with a particular method in mind, perhaps imagining he was in control of events within the room and consuming what he needed to continue on his path. But that sounded like more of the psychobabble Jane had always talked about. Lazy assumptions based on conjecture. He was probably enjoying the taste and saving the larger part of the ginger body until last. Didn't most of us work around the edges before taking on the main tasks in life?

'What sort of work is that?' Lanning asked, picking up another Garibaldi while eyeing a gingerbread man. Would he look indulgent and unprofessional picking one of those? Garibaldis were safe and dry with a hint of sweetness. It felt wrong to be thinking of biscuits when a trauma patient was about to offer something new. It was wrong. Damn the biscuits.

'She asked me to write some copy for her latest campaign. It's freelance but very well paid.'

'That sounds interesting and focused. How are you finding it?'

Lanning became aware he hadn't followed up Catherine's gardening information with any questions. He wrote a quick C G on his pad and waited for Patrick to finish chewing.

'It's really ... boring. Really bloody boring. I want to get it finished and get on with an idea I've had.'

Lanning nodded. He wanted to know what the idea was but knew he had to ask Catherine about her gardening. It was too easy to allow any one of them to take over the session on one note, usually it was either Patrick or himself. Catherine was highly considerate of talking space and time. She always seemed to underuse the opportunities. Perhaps that was part of her survival mechanism, to keep the atmosphere as light as her mind and body needed to get through each day.

'I'd like to hear about your idea. It sounds interesting. But I would like to hear about Catherine's gardening first. Have you been planting or maintaining?'

Lanning knew his statement and question was akin to a talk-show host. He imagined Jane, standing in the corner of the room, shaking her head, with a look of incredulity on her face, mouthing *What was that?*

Catherine had picked up a gingerbread man. She had started with the head too. She smiled at Lanning. Her front teeth were covered in biscuit bits. Everything about her face seemed to be changing as she ate more. Her smile seemed to be wild, as if she was thinking of biting Lanning's head off soon.

Lanning picked up the last gingerbread man, bit his head off, chewing it as if he hadn't eaten in hours, and smiled back at Catherine, pushing biscuit against his front teeth. He was unnerved but excited at the shift in behaviour, feeling connected, following behaviour which might allow them all to finally move through formality.

'Planting all sorts', Catherine said. She licked her fingers.

She sat back and crossed her arms. Patrick did the same.

'Have you been gardening regularly?' Lanning asked, glancing at the remains of his gingerbread man and berating himself for not leaving some tea to wash it down with.

Catherine didn't answer. Lanning waited for a few seconds, wondering whether she might be finishing her biscuit or thinking about something specific relating to her time with plants. But she was staring at him then at Patrick then back at him, as if she were a robot stuck in a programming loop glitch.

'Are you feeling all right?' Lanning posed the question at Catherine but, having noticed Patrick doing the same staring back and forth motions, was asking both of them. He waited again.

'Would you like to take a break?'

More staring and silence.

'All right. Are you both feeling annoyed about something, with me? Or is this rather odd behaviour change part of an elaborate joke?'

Lanning breathed deeply but felt his face getting warmer. He had high blood pressure and always tried to stay as calm as possible but this situation was making him angry and on edge. He wanted to shout at them, tell them to behave and act with respect in his house, that he was in charge and they should do as he told them to do, to follow the rules as he chose them.

'It's not very nice, is it?' Patrick said, sitting forward and pulling his chair closer towards Catherine.

20

'Do you feel concerned about us, scared that we've become people you hardly recognise or know?' Catherine continued. She pulled her chair towards Patrick, until they were side by side, arm touching arm.

Lanning didn't understand anything. He felt bullied and terrified, as if they were going to hurt him, that they had lost their minds along the way without him noticing any change at all, becoming one mind of traumatic psychosis, that he was a fraud and a fool who had played with fire from the start and now his life was about to be completely immolated. Madness was in the air.

'What are you talking about? Please tell me if you have a grievance with me or the work we're doing?' he said, aware his throat was dry and his voice sounded reedy and weak. 'This is getting very strange. Perhaps we should end the session a bit early?'

'Do you want us to forget the whole thing, doc, not bother coming back?' Patrick leaned back.

Lanning half-expected him to sling his arm around Catherine's shoulders; perhaps they would show him their vampire smiles soon, lips licked with gingerbread and blood, just before they drained his neck. At least he might get to see Jane again and find rest in the endlessness.

Lanning had always managed to remain calm in times of great stress at the hospital — if a patient had a psychotic break or he was faced with a particularly emotionally damaged person unleashing their pain. He had remained calm when Jane died and organised arrangements for her funeral and a Christian burial, even finding the capacity to talk through flower arrangement placements with the vicar, deciding a range of various types of irises would have been Jane's choice. But now he felt as if he would lose his calm, watch himself in the reflection of the framed Dali print behind his desk as the anxiety growing inside became too hot to withstand and his limbs became ash, dropping away, followed by his torso and most of his face, until he was only a twisted and open mouth, unable to articulate anything, left with a low howl until there was nothing.

'We've been coming here for weeks now, telling you everything you've wanted to hear. What have you given us?'

Lanning didn't understand a word of anything. Catherine had clearly paused, waiting for him to say something, but he just nodded as if she had offered some new part of her narrative and was deciding where to go to next.

'I understand, please go on', he said.

'It took so much for us to enter into this, and you were right to start the process, but we thought it was going to be *shared* therapy. We share, but you don't, *at all*. That's not fair, is it?'

Catherine looked at Patrick who was holding her hand now and nodding quickly in support.

Why are they holding hands, Lanning thought, are they lovers?

'I ... what do you mean?' he said. His voice sounded slow, each word pronounced with care.

'You bring us into your home, feed us coffee and biscuits, even taking the time to give us gingerbread men, I'm guessing you were listening in on us discussing them last week. But you don't reveal anything. You talk about authenticity in our memories and allowing ourselves to be true. We may as well be talking to an empty chair. Who the hell are *you*?'

Patrick's voice seemed to have gained volume and speed. He was eating a Garibaldi. Lanning noticed there was only one left.

'If I've given you both less than one hundred per cent of my attention, I'm terribly sorry. I never meant to give the impression of that. What more can I say?'

'You can tell us about you'. Catherine sat forward and took Lanning's hand. 'Tell us what's happened to you and brought you to us. I've seen all the photographs of that woman. You're hiding them and you're hiding from us. We've decided if you

20

won't *share* with us, we won't be coming back to share anything else with you. We want to try other ways.'

Catherine stood up first. She let go of Lanning's hand and held Patrick's again.

After they had left the house, Lanning sat and stared at his mobile phone home screen photograph of Jane. He remembered holding her hand, on the sofa watching television or a film, walking through the local fields or in bed after making love. He realised no one had touched him for such a long time.

21

Catherine couldn't bring herself to ask Patrick in for a cup of tea. She felt exhausted and guilty, about the trap they had sprung on Lanning and about her mix of feelings for Patrick and how they might become amplified inside the house she had bought with Harry.

'*Did* we do the right thing with Lanning?' she said.

'Yes, we did. He isn't being honest. We're telling all our private thoughts and he's still a stranger.'

Catherine smiled but imagined Lanning sobbing, staring at one of the photographs of the mysterious woman, still sitting where they had left him, feeling as if he had completely failed. But he *had* already helped them. She was beginning to imagine the future without Harry, in small parts but more regularly — her next birthday and Christmas morning without him, going on a holiday or choosing new clothes. Nothing huge but enough to remember he had always been there with her.

Patrick had become essential to her, not in any romantic fashion, none of that. She wouldn't want to think about another relationship yet, but he *did* feel like a partner in some vital part of her life. They talked and sent each other texts throughout the day — GIFs, silly observations and, lately, ideas about things they had always wanted to do and not do, but had previously felt compromised by being in a committed relationship, including neither of them wanting children. Patrick told her Maggie had threatened to leave him unless he agreed to have one.

'I think I knew she would say that and secretly wanted her to go', he had said, looking away from Catherine, as if he still felt the cold dash of exposed shame across his face.

Catherine had lied to Harry about wanting to have his babies. Should she feel even more shame than Patrick? Surely it was always worse to lead someone along a path, with

21

them joyously visualising a future predicated on a total lie. And what would she have done if they had gone ahead and had children, would she have held her newborn and felt the parental connection initiate, or instead her fingers lock in the blind panic of realising she had created another person without love. Was caring for a new life you didn't want worse than starting an old one alone?

Harry was from a large Catholic family and had virtually insisted they try for at least three 'small ones', as he insisted on calling them, Catherine didn't need reminding how small they would be, that only added to her anxiety. Harry gave them names, after too much wine when they had friends over for dinner. They were all so young but two couples had already got married and had a child together. What was the rush?

'Jack, Rose and Niamh. Yeah, Niamh, you know, like Cath's friend from work. It's pronounced Neeve. I love that name. No, it wouldn't be weird having the same name as a friend. It wouldn't be weird. You're weird, you weirdo...'

His happy voice would become louder with each syllable and her head would spin with the terror she felt about being pregnant, feeling forever held back in her life, as if she was being told how her freedom in the decades ahead had already been given over to parenthood. Had she resented him for that? Had she wished him away?

Patrick talked about the many ways he had allowed Maggie to dictate terms in their marriage. He usually admitted his own culpability and laziness in decision making, saying he had disliked himself more than her for not saying how he wanted his life to be.

'I know this sounds unusual, and *obviously* I wish Maggie was still alive, but something about being alone again feels exciting, as if I have an opportunity to begin everything again. Do you ever feel something similar, something quite separate from the loss of Harry?'

Catherine had said she wasn't really certain of anything like that, but she was. She knew she had been given opportunity as well as pain. Losing someone created an empty space, but it was possible, in time, to fill that space with things that might make you feel alive again, things where you might find a different version of joy.

'Would you do me a favour?' Patrick said, as he was turning to leave Catherine at her front door.

'Sure. What's that?'

'Would you imagine some things that are considered taboo, a bit odd, that blur the lines of what's supposed to be wrong and right, not necessarily breaking any laws. Things you might want to do in a world where they might be thought of as okay and usual?'

'When you say *taboo* are you talking about ... sex?'

Patrick looked surprised then smiled.

'Not that, no.'

'I will do. But why?'

'I'll show you mine when you're ready to show me yours', Patrick said and laughed. Catherine rolled her eyes and shook her head, holding up her hand as a goodbye.

He had closed the front garden gate as slowly and considerately as ever, checking the latch was down. He saluted and walked away. Catherine wondered about him, how he always seemed so organised and settled in himself and his thoughts.

She spent some time writing a list of potential taboo ideas, she crossed out most of them as either too boring or too sexual. She sat and stared at the armchair Harry had made his own, trying to remember whether they had ever touched upon ideas considered to blur the lines of right and wrong. She couldn't think of anything. In fact, the more she thought about the things they had talked about and done in the last few years, the more she wondered whether they would have lasted as a couple. Harry's work as a solicitor was taking away a lot of their evening and weekend time — he had been promoted quickly and was assisting one of the partners in the employment law department.

'The work feels real. It feels as if I'm genuinely helping people to get what they deserve and not be ripped off by some scumbag boss. I know we were going to see your parents but they live so close and we do see them all the time. You go, and give them my love. I'm sure they'll understand I have to work. Okay?'

But it hadn't been okay. It wasn't okay that time or all the other times he had cancelled something at the last minute. Or in other situations, such as when she had forgotten her house key, sent him a text to leave work on time to let her in and found herself waiting for an hour and a half because he had been in an important meeting. Wasn't *she* supposed to be the most important thing to him? He wanted her to be the mother of his Jack, Rose and Niamh. Surely that should be on her list?

She had begun to feel as if she was becoming single again quite some time before the accident. Had she been unreasonable? Had she complained too much? She had always been happy to see him, to know he was there. Why hadn't that been enough, was she a bad person?

Perhaps one of the taboo subjects on her list should be thinking *difficult* thoughts about Harry. Did that count as taboo or blurring the lines of right and wrong? Quite possibly when that person is dead and can't include you on their own list. Perhaps she would have been at the top of Harry's.

22

Patrick had already started writing his list of the things he wanted to do and not do. He had included: Go back in time and never meet and marry Maggie.

Would he tell that one to Catherine?

The making of the list might be considered a taboo in itself. But to wonder about the morality of the content seemed antithetical to the idea of writing it. He should be allowed to write what he wanted, even if no one ever saw it.

Would he edit a diluted copy to read for Catherine? What if she was writing her version this very minute, opening her soul to every previously withheld emotion and desire, only to discover he had been an absolute coward in his offering. He had to be honest and write *everything*, even the most abhorrent ideas, including the worst one relating to the details of how he would eradicate any sign he had ever known someone called Maggie. Was it possible to divorce someone after they've died?

His favourite idea, the one which he had wondered about over many recent years, was to find the gang of three morons who had bullied him for the first two and a half years of secondary school and have his revenge — mental and physical tortures followed by their gory deaths. While the actual memories of their violence and threats towards him had faded, the hatred he felt for them was as deep and wide now as it had been then. More so, as he had been too terrified in those days to find the headspace, or nerves, for hatred or any idea he would ever be in a position to get back at them.

One of the morons had, inconsiderately, already died. Patrick had seen his obituary in the local newspaper, just over a year before. The moron had been a champion weightlifter — surely that title was an *oxymoron* — Patrick had laughed out loud when he saw the death announcement and lied to Maggie about the hilarious content. She wouldn't have understood it. The theme of vengeance was completely opposed to her live and let live views.

Would it be considered too weird to ask a question on his list, something to get a second opinion on, about finding out where the dead moron's family lived and enacting some kind of revenge upon them — a vengeance by proxy? They had raised him and were, in part, responsible for the streak of cruelty that had made him crush the hope and happiness out of the young Patrick, and a lot of other boys. Someone deserved to pay for that. That would definitely make the list.

He felt a new energy in his abilities, liberated in the realisation he could begin to track down the surviving bullies. He had been given *life itself* after the crash, a new place in the world, new eyes and time to use them again, to clear the murk from his previously compliant and dull existence.

Leigh Evans was a builder now. His LinkedIn page had him listed as a: *Building Maintenance Technician and Managing Supervisor*. That title would be quite the mouthful for Leigh, a tall, wide and brutal boy at school who could barely say a sentence without including *wanker* or *fuck*. Patrick grinned as he looked at Evans' sullen, point-blank face on screen. There was sunshine all around the photograph but Evans couldn't bring himself to smile or drop the tough guy image.

He had always maintained the same dull-headed look, that life was pain and he would give out more than he had ever taken. Perhaps he had been abused as a child. Patrick gave that a moment and decided he didn't care.

Evans only laughed at school when there was violence and intimidation. Even then he seemed to be faking enjoyment, as if he instinctively knew it was expected of him. Patrick wondered whether Evans was still a thug, had allowed his tendencies to grow and spill out into the adult world, learning he had to be more careful as he got older — a prison sentence was very different to a week of school suspension. Patrick allowed his mind to run into the wilds of hunting something, balancing the scales of his own justice.

Evans was probably a serial killer now, using his tools and building site work to make his victims disappear. There were probably lots of concrete graves and well-cleaned claw hammers. Did he have a particular type of victim, would they all look like Patrick?

If that was true, how was it feasible someone as stupid as Evans could get away with multiple murders? Was it really that easy to kill with impunity?

Patrick began to feel uneasy looking at Evans' face. His dead eyes still managed to chill Patrick's blood and make him anxious. How was that possible? Would those emotional scars never heal?

Patrick wondered if he should send a text or call Catherine, asking for her thoughts on the way he had begun to think and feel. Lanning might be the better option. Although he still had ground to make up, he was a psychiatrist and would certainly have experience to offer.

He decided against contacting either of them. This was still about his list, his desires and the wonderment of *choice*. These were thoughts not actions, they were free to him. He was allowed to think anything he wanted. He wasn't a murderer.

The last moron had been a short boy with a shorter temper. Dean Clift had been the leader of the trio, the one who seemed to relish finding new ways to inflict the worst kind of humiliation on Patrick, including boxing him in at the back of the top section of seats on a school bus and making him take his trousers off to leave when it was his stop.

Patrick found him on Facebook.

There were multiple posts from Dean. All of them were predictable: Dean at the Silverstone Grand Prix; Dean in Ibiza; Dean grinning inanely in a cheap three-piece suit with a bunch

22

of equally grim-looking men, perhaps at a wedding or funeral. Dean had children now. Did he hurt and humiliate them? Or was he a doting father, someone who had become a version of a good person; would he have killed to protect those children? There was no redemption for anyone like him. He had done enough harm, by the age of 16, to last a lifetime. Any children of his would carry the same diseased brain.

'You've always been a thick, loser bastard', Patrick whispered, realising he could say anything, at any volume, these days. Maggie wasn't there to reproach him anymore, telling him he needed to find ways to access his zen, or something like that. 'You should both be dead, too, just like your steroid pushing friend', he shouted, feeling his hands clench until his knuckles turned white.

23

Lanning cancelled the weekly session, sending texts to Catherine and Patrick saying he was unwell and apologising. He offered them an additional session during the following week and reassured them he was still available by email or telephone at any time.

He hoped they wouldn't call him. He wasn't ready to hear their voices again, not yet. He didn't go into the hospital either, telling them the same lie about his health. Why shouldn't he take some time off? He hadn't taken a holiday for over two years and only a few days after Jane died. The thought of time off seemed like an invitation for grief, an opportunity for his heart to slow and eventually decide it couldn't be bothered to go on without Jane's presence to quicken it again and keep it pumping. He knew he was on borrowed hours and days.

But there was still work to be done. What was left of his life could be used to continue helping Catherine and Patrick. All he needed was a few days to regroup his energy for the work and rethink his approach. There were always moments like the other day, patients becoming disenchanted or angry, doubting the veracity of the worth in their psychiatrist. He had felt that himself, with his peers attending review sessions, asking questions which made him want to throw them out of the nearest window. The science of the mind was as volatile as nitroglycerin. He had been wounded, was confused but still able to breathe and focus and begin his notes for the next session. Perhaps he had felt ashamed by their behaviour going unchallenged by him, in his home, with Jane everywhere.

His stammer had returned. Not as badly as it had plagued his childhood and early adulthood, but enough to make him restart the practice techniques he had learned during a hard nineteen months of speech therapy — compartmentalising his thoughts and slowly sounding out each syllable. Other children were often cruel and made fun of him. The older he became, embarrassment among his peers replaced mocking. The most abject moments were those when, well-meaning though they were, friends and family would make extreme lip shapes to encourage him, often finishing his sentences with words he hadn't intended, then nodding and smiling at him as if he was lesser than them and akin to a toddler forming primary language.

Stress always made things worse. When he was in the early stages of asking Jane out, he could barely summon the fortitude required to put enough fluency together to approach her. That felt like pure agony — the desire to be poetic smashed by the reality of his mouth twisting and stretching to say something as simple as Thank You.

'I can say anything I choose to say in any given moment and situation. I am in control of my own, unique voice. My favourite word in the entire English language is mellifluous. Mellifluous. Mell...if...luo...us', Lanning said the words slowly and carefully, looking at himself, specifically his face, mouth then eyes then mouth again, in the hallway mirror. He needed to shave and wash his hair but that would have to wait.

Lanning spent hours talking things through with Jane. He would lose himself in conversation with her, not breaking his dialogue when he completed the most mundane task, such as going to the toilet or making a cup of tea. He needed to regain his initial desire to complete the shared therapy and begin to map out what he wanted to gain from its completion. He hadn't started all of this from the goodness of his heart. He was still a professional who was planning a wide-ranging research paper, perhaps a book too, as his comeback. He might be given a department head position at the university — Professor Lanning sounded overdue. He had been called doctor for a long time and a change, an upgraded change, would have made Jane so very proud.

'I've always had so much faith in you, and I'm so very proud of all you've achieved. Your book is simply marvellous, my darling. You saved those two people from despair and loneliness. You're an angel. My angel.'

She might have said those exact words. Lanning knew she was still watching him, giving him the courage to carry on.

Lanning sent Catherine and Patrick texts confirming the next session. In honesty, he didn't feel absolutely ready to see them again, but he wasn't sure he ever would, Did he even like them? It wasn't necessary to feel positively about any patient, but it often helped. Catherine was someone he could imagine talking to outside of a therapeutic setting, enjoying her opinions and laughter. But Patrick was a cold one, a person who Lanning had been unable to read or begin to get the measure of. He seemed compassionate, and was very protective and solicitous of Catherine. He did listen to Lanning and hadn't ever challenged him, before the previous session, but his eyes and facial movements seemed to indicate he was, as his mother used to refer to one of his university friends, *a shifty sod*.

Lanning had felt protective of Catherine when Patrick had taken her hand, even though he had felt under attack from both of them at the time. He imagined he might have felt the same way if Catherine was his daughter.

'Am I getting too close to all of this to be objective?' he whispered to a photograph of Jane standing next to the Eiffel Tower.

Her eyes were wide open, in awe of the construction. She seemed to be exploding with joy in that moment, overwhelmed by the city and him. He closed his eyes and felt tears begin to form.

'I miss you so much. It all feels too much, too much time.'

23

He deliberately gave them start times fifteen minutes apart, hoping they would arrive separately, allowing him a much needed pause and opportunity to see how they behaved without the other person as a back-up. But they were both standing on the driveway when he opened the front door. They were already laughing and closely chatting, seeming to be sharing a private joke. Was *he* the punchline?

'I think you must be losing your mind, doc', Patrick said, shaking Lanning's hand and grinning.

'Hello, Patrick. Hi Catherine. How am I losing my mind?' Lanning wanted to slap Patrick's grin away.

'You gave us different start times.'

Lanning brought the coffee tray through to his study. He had put a small pile of older biscuits on a plate, having found them in a tin at the bottom of a food storage cupboard. He recognised the chipped Bourbons and dusty custard creams. He didn't know how old they were and was determined not to eat any or give them another thought. Catherine and Patrick could play lucky dip with them for all he cared.

'How's your garden, Catherine?' he said.

Catherine raised her eyebrows and nodded as if she were appraising his question before answering.

'It's good, fine. But let's all be honest, we need to talk about the last time we were here, about why that happened and what we should do next. What do you think?'

Catherine looked at Patrick. He smiled at her and held the look for a few seconds. Lanning thought about stepping in immediately, laying his own law down and telling them to either play along or get the hell out, but that sounded petulant and, breaking a golden rule of psychiatry, becoming emotionally involved. He breathed slowly and managed to smile as beneficently as he could while he waited for Patrick to opine.

'That says it all, I think, doc. Really well put. We've been talking, and we want to know more about you, who you are. You listen to us, you know our intimate details, who our families and friends are, and we don't know you at all. That's not a healthy balance, is it? And we want to talk about how we move forward. We only seem to talk about how everything relates to our pasts.'

Lanning's immediate response might have been to remind them both how the past informs the present and the future, and without facing unresolved issues and trauma the healing process and making any true progress would be impossible. But he guessed they might be waiting for him to say something like that, relishing a prepared retort at his expense, rendering him a fraud, a has-been. Forget it, he thought, I'm done with falling into traps. Say what you need to say.

He nodded and waited, looking Patrick in the eye, attempting to seem engaged, unthreatened and open to suggestions.

Catherine spoke next. Lanning knew right then, they had organised the sequence of this opening salvo.

'Are you married, or divorced?'

'I was married.'

Lanning's right hand tightened around his pen. They wouldn't be able to see that.

'Do you still see your ex-wife?' Patrick asked.

Lanning hadn't been comfortable with Catherine's question but hadn't felt any animosity towards her for asking. But there was something about Patrick's tone that sounded as if he somehow doubted Lanning's own past and was trying to establish a position of authority.

'Only in photographs.'

'Did she remarry?' Catherine asked. She leaned forwards, into a pose of support and understanding. Jane had done the same thing when she was beginning to reach out to him, knowing he would soon need her hand to keep him standing.

'No. She died. She's dead.'

Silence dropped. They all sat still, not looking at each other. Lanning wasn't sure how he felt.

'May I ask when she passed away', Patrick said. His voice sounded contrite.

'I'd rather not refer to it as *passing away*. She died. She stopped breathing and her heart stopped. That happened some months ago. May *I* ask how this is important for you to know? I understand we all have a natural curiosity about other people's lives but I don't think you knowing about my marital status is part of the process we've begun.'

Catherine and Patrick looked at each other again.

'Thank you, Christopher', Catherine said.

'You're welcome, Catherine', Lanning replied, happy to hear her use his name. He excluded Patrick from his warmth and focused his attention only on her. He wondered whether Jane would have chided him for being too hard. He looked at his patients and noticed their faces looked relaxed, their jawlines looser. He wasn't an expert in micro expressions but was glad of any sign things might go easier on him. He had a small list of areas he wanted to begin to cover with them, areas he hoped might interest them and which, if they picked up a link between themselves and his grief, could allow him to be more open. But he wouldn't force anything. It *did* feel good to share about Jane, to connect more with these remarkable people, these fellow survivors, and although he still didn't completely like or trust Patrick, or his influence on Catherine, he did understand what had happened to the younger man's life — the denial, the change, the force of impact on his emotions — had clearly embedded trauma into him as deeply as it could ever go.

'We've been talking about the way the sessions are run and we would like to offer suggestions for change. Are you open to that?' Catherine said. She spoke very quickly, looking at Lanning, seemingly in a rush, unblinking and holding something which looked like her own list. He had expected conversations to shift but not this, another move against his authority.

'I'm open to listening to anything you want to say, of course', he said. He could feel his own jawline tightening now and wondered whether either of them knew about micro expressions. He wanted to throw his list at the wall, walk to the kitchen, open the freezer and down the remains of the half bottle of vodka.

'Good stuff. Thanks, doc', Patrick said, giving a thumbs-up as if Lanning had succeeded in the first of a series of challenges. Was he *really* expected to fight for his position in the room. *His room.*

'Feel free to share your ideas', he said, turning the page on his own ideas and raising his pen, ready to copy down whatever Catherine and Patrick had decided the session work should become. With two against one and his need to continue his research and follow this process back to the surface of his reputation, Lanning knew he didn't have any choice now. He wasn't the leader anymore. He was a willing follower, a standing guest who would chronicle them, occasionally asking questions to elicit more information. Maybe that would prove to be enough, maybe not. Would that actually help them, or him?

Did any of it matter anymore? As Catherine began reading from her notes, talking about how she and Patrick were determined to break their old conventions of conforming to expectations, not being specific about how they would do that, he guessed he would be expected to produce the psychological kindling. One of Jane's favourite quotes ran through his head: 'Sometimes those who are lost do not realise and live as if they were never found at all.'

24

Catherine woke up absolutely certain she could hear Harry singing in the shower. His pillow felt warm and was depressed as if his head had recently lifted away from it. She wasn't sure what she would say to him when he came back to the bedroom. Had she dreamed his death, like some cheesy soap opera? Things seemed normal in the house. She remembered a poem about dreaming in another dream used in a song by a German band. Was that happening to her?

She got out of bed, looked through a crack in the curtain; the street was quiet, nothing to increase any sense of the subconscious world having invaded.

The shower and singing had stopped, and the bathroom was empty when she opened the door. She used the toilet and stared at the rail opposite, realising Harry's Batman towel and flannel set were still there; bone dry, the edges curling up and hardened. They needed to go. Would his parents want them? They had given them to him as a humorous present when he got his offer at university. She wouldn't do that, it would be tactless and insensitive, Harry was their only child. Did they blame her for his death? Was she responsible?

When she had woken up in the hospital and begun the process of working with Lanning, she had focused on her feelings about her injuries and losing Harry, how she felt in any given moment. And since beginning the shared therapy, she had talked about how her life had been affected by the traumas involved in someone so close having gone forever, how her life might have been different and, again, how she felt in any given moment. But the thing she wanted to remember the most, to talk about until she collapsed from the pain of full recognition, was the night of the crash — how everything had come to pass, who she had been in the moments before, during and after Harry had died. Her physical pain after the crash didn't mean anything now. She had been very lucky, only suffering some broken bones, two deep cuts needing stitches and a mild concussion. Her left shoulder had taken some time to get rid of the red welt from the extreme pull of the seatbelt, but the airbag had prevented her from being obliterated. She had been told Harry died from the severity of a side impact hit.

Catherine folded the Batman towel and flannel and didn't know where to put them. She walked across the landing and opened Harry's wardrobe. They could live in there for now. The smell of deodorant on his clothing was still there. It made her lean in, her face between two sleeves. She breathed in through her nose a few times and rested her cheek against the arm of his favourite blue linen summer jacket.

Niamh had sent her a text about the possibility of meeting later that day. She wondered again whether their boss had tasked her best friend with encouraging her back to work. The last time she met Niamh there had been a lot of mentions relating to the work place, the in-jokes, the future projects newly arrived and how very much everyone missed Catherine. At the time she had felt nostalgic for her work friends, the daily routine of satisfaction in her job and knowing she was good at what she did. But since discussing her list of unusual desires and thoughts — the deviance list, as she had decided to call it — with Patrick, she had cared less and less about her career, and the thought of listening to Niamh press her, unsubtly, about a return to work made her hands clench and a clear message go through her mind: goodbye to all of that...

She sent back a reply: Hi sweetie, I can't make tonight. Not feeling well. I'll text you when I'm doing better xx.

Niamh responded quickly: Okay, lovely. We all miss you. Speak soon xxxxxx.

Niamh always overdid the kisses and the group-think sentiment.

24

Catherine took her deviance list out from the back of the latest novel she was reading and looked at it. It seemed so tame, not deviant in the slightest. Her top desire was still: *tell people talking in the cinema, during a film, to shut up.* She wrote, above the cinema pests: *punch someone for being rude.* That felt right, like justice, like deviance.

She rewrote the whole list quickly, feeling a new will surge through her, an anger towards so much of her previous life, what it was, what it might have become and how she had been deluded into thinking she was happy with it. She had done so much and enjoyed so little, worrying all the time about losing out on opportunities to be content, then losing everything and finding out she may have been wanting something else all the time. Nothing was clear anymore, she didn't have any true idea of who she might want to be, and she liked that feeling. She was beginning to fall in love with it.

25

Patrick watched Leigh Evans walk out of the small café holding a paper cup of something hot, steam rising from the surface. He waved back into the café and laughed, saying something Patrick couldn't hear.

Patrick had correctly assumed Evans' listed business address was also his home and waited for him, arriving as anonymously as he could manage, parking some way along the road and lying low in his car. He remained mostly still throughout the night, as if he was on a stake-out, bored and cold, intermittently falling asleep, and waking each time with a start of panic that he might have missed Evans leaving the house. Each time he woke he drank more coffee from his flask, using one of the two empty litre plastic bottles he had packed when he needed to empty his bladder.

Patrick's asthma seemed to be a bit worse when the sun began to rise. He took a puff of Salbutamol and washed his mouth around with water. He used some of the water to bathe his eyes, one of them was sore from a lack of rest. He had made too many cheese and tomato sandwiches and couldn't face another one even though he was hungry. He wasn't sure what he wanted to do about anything now that daylight had begun to expose the world in full, but he couldn't leave yet. Catherine had sent him two texts in the night — one saying she had rewritten her list, her *deviant list*, the other wishing him sweet dreams. She had added three kisses to the second text, it was the first time she had done that. He felt elated to see them, immediately more awake and energetic to whatever might happen on this new day. But he didn't have a plan of any sort. Finding Evans had been a spontaneous decision which had felt so right as he sat looking at his LinkedIn profile photograph again, the fourth day in succession of returning to the site.

Meeting Evans again had taken the top spot in his new ideas. He hadn't given the list a name yet and thought Catherine's was symbolic of her beautiful nature, especially when she admitted her number one desire was asking some blabbermouth in the cinema to shut up.

'That *is* big, for me', she had said loudly, laughing with him. He had pretended to cower away, looking at her face and wondering how he could ever be good enough for her. Wherever they might be heading together wasn't necessarily about romantic love. It was about protection, taking the force of any blows that might come towards either of them, looking out for Catherine and allowing her to have the best life she could have.

Evans waved through the café window one more time and returned to his white van, placing his hot drink inside and checking the ladder on the roof. His name and business details were printed on the sides of the van in red and yellow.

White Van Man, still a fucking cliché, Patrick thought. He wanted to buy a bacon sandwich, anything edible, from the café, but Evans was about to drive away. Hunger would have to wait, coming second to a new obsession, a sense of justice empowered at last, even if it was beginning to feel akin to something pointless.

Evans' day was almost as boring as Patrick's. He made, what looked like, some residential maintenance visits and seemed to continuously eat and drink. He was a heavier build than Patrick had imagined, slower too, but still looked physically dangerous. Even from a distance he had the presence of a man who could give and take a lot of violence, a resting face of malevolence.

As Patrick was attempting to fall asleep, in his own bed, having returned to his home a few hours before, his mind felt full of possibilities, most of them being blown to pieces as soon as they began to stand up. What could he really do to hurt Evans? How far was he willing to go to take revenge seriously?

Patrick took three days to decide where to start with Evans — hurt him by hurting his business, his income. It would be lovely to beat the thug into submission, punish him and make him cry out for mercy, and that could happen soon too, but Patrick wanted to make Evans really feel the weight of his cruelty and be more contrite than he could have imagined.

Evans was clearly and absolutely reliant on his van. Patrick had seen enough of his daily travels to know he worked alone and needed the utility vehicle to carry himself, his tools and his pathetic public image to each client. He would be able to hire a replacement van, but the hit to his credibility and sense of efficiency was a wonderful way to start, and van hire was expensive. When that stage was complete, Patrick would begin on the next one — perhaps he could find a way to cut the power to Evans' house or cause a gas explosion, create some method of damaging his entire life, or ending it?

Patrick parked in a different spot, further down the road from Evans' front door. He watched his enemy leave for work, checking his roof ladders again. That seemed like a compulsion, maybe it was some sort of health and safety measure the moron had learned about his so-called skill set.

Evans had no right to the further education and training he would have required for his job after working with the other morons and systematically destroying Patrick's opportunities at secondary school and directly contributing to his appalling exam results and stalled life — going back to re-sit courses, missing his time achieving A-levels, crushing his confidence with women and setting his social skill level at a firm basic. Any hope of going to university had been put so far into the distance that Patrick only ever thought of it as something other people did. He had worked with a few colleagues who seemed mystified to discover he didn't have a degree, then saying he should *definitely* get one. Smiling and shrugging that assumption away each time was a different level of pain and reminder of his past.

Patrick shook his head slowly and snorted in derision, thinking about this most-hated person worrying about potential accidents and harm to other people. He didn't seem capable of anything so altruistic. He was probably just concerned with being sued or having to buy new ladders.

They were obviously of great value to Evans. Patrick decided to destroy or steal them — perhaps he would knock out every other rung, that might send a just message about balance.

He wanted a last look at the routine parts in Evans' day, any additional ways he could inflict pain and upset. But there wasn't anything to see. Evans visited the café for his morning beverage and laugh, ate junk food excessively and made house calls to fix toilet seats and unblock drains.

This man is the walking dead, as mundane and directionless as I knew he would be, Patrick thought. If I didn't hate him, I might feel sorry for him. Perhaps allowing him to live and feel the accumulation of existential self-hatred and the waste of his life is worse than anything I could do to him?

But that wasn't true. This wasn't about the cause or effect of any action on the existence of Leigh Evans; Patrick had doubts about the man's ability to feel anything nearing philosophical angst. This was about the power of retribution, of making another person see themselves the way you have seen them, feeling the fear the way you have felt it, realising the past never dies, it just waits around life-corners to catch up with you.

The hand on his shoulder was obviously Evans' but Patrick took a moment to pray it might be Catherine's.

'What the fuck are you doing, mate?' Evans said. His raspy voice was different, deeper from cigarettes (Patrick had counted Evans smoking at least ten in one day), but still horribly recognisable.

'I dropped my mobile under your van', Patrick replied slowly; his heart was racing and his mouth was dry but he was determined not to be overwhelmed by fear. He smiled at Evans, even though he wanted to spit in his face.

'Is that it?' Evans said, stepping slightly back and squinting at Patrick.

'What would *it* be?' Patrick forced his smile to grow wider. He wanted to lick his lips and swallow but fixed his smile.

'Do you really think I haven't seen you watching me?'

Patrick's stomach dropped.

'Why would I be watching you?'

Evans smiled and leaned on his van. He pulled cigarettes from his top pocket and lit one.

'I remember you. It took me a while, but I recognise your face properly now. You're Patrick something, that guy from school. Why are you watching me, and what were you going to do to my van?'

Patrick wanted to both run at Evans and launch himself, at full speed, into a frenzied attack, and also to run away as fast as he could. Evans had forgotten his surname. Surely Hawton wasn't that difficult to remember? It wasn't Smith or Brown, but it was distinct, or should be, especially when you've victimised that person.

Patrick shrugged and smiled. He hadn't accounted for this scenario and wasn't ready to improvise. He felt a numbness in his legs.

'I dropped my mobile and was searching for it. I don't know who you are and I haven't been *watching* you or anyone else. You have a good day, pal.'

Patrick turned around and began to walk away. He felt Evans's hand on his shoulder again. This time it spun him around and pushed his back against the van.

'Hawthorn? That's your name, isn't it?' Evans said. He was showing his teeth and holding Patrick flat against the driver's

25

door. 'I remember you. You were always a little twat. Did you fancy me at school? Is that why you're here, to tell me you've been in love with me all these years?'

Patrick knew he should be terrified, but he was thinking of Maggie, how appalled she would be he had allowed himself to become involved in stalking someone and this threat of violence. That made him happy, that he had confounded her idea of him, even though she wasn't there to witness it. He had finally risen up and followed his instincts instead of meekly encouraging life to keep pushing him around.

'That's right, Leigh. I love you. I love you. I want *you*', Patrick shouted the last three words and leaned forward, pretending he was trying to kiss Evans, smacking his lips.

Evans pushed him back against the door. Patrick slipped to one side and hit his ear on the large wing mirror.

'Stay down, you freak', Evans sounded exactly the same as he had at secondary school — savage and uncaring, as if Patrick's life had no meaning other than giving him the pleasure of administering pain upon.

Patrick twisted his body and pushed forward, using his hands to punch Evans' armpits. The larger man registered the blow, his face bunched into a moment of pain. He stood back and stared at Patrick in disbelief.

'You're scum. You always were and you always will be', Patrick said. He breathed in and wondered whether Catherine would be proud of him, and what Lanning might say.

Patrick seemed to see Evans' fist and feel the connection of it at the same time. It took some seconds for the impact to become pain, which felt like aching and heat all over his head. Patrick felt liquid on his lips, guessing it was either snot or blood. His ear was throbbing and he had fallen to his knees.

'If I see you around here again, I'll bury you alive', Evans whispered into Patrick's painful ear. His mouth was close enough to smell his rancid breath. 'Now, fuck off.'

Patrick struggled to open his car door. His mouth tasted as if it was full of blood. One of his eyes was partially closed and his ribs were agony whenever he took a breath. He knew he should probably call an ambulance but he wanted to sleep. He was exhausted. He had seen Evans drive away. Perhaps he could rest for a while then go home.

26

Lanning wanted to ask Patrick why he had a black eye, what had happened, and did it have anything to do with the therapy. He looked at the younger man, breathing in and out slowly, barely containing the pain he was clearly feeling all over his body. Was it something so simple as an accident? Self-harming? Was he professionally obliged to ask Patrick, perhaps later, after the session, in private, what was going on?

Catherine looked worried. She sipped her coffee and glanced at Patrick then fake-smiled at Lanning.

'How are you both? Actually, in light of what we were talking about recently, perhaps I should tell you how *I* am?'

Lanning waited a beat for any disapproval then continued.

'I've had a tough week. I've been thinking about my wife ... Jane, a lot. I sometimes talk to her photographs, the way I used to talk to her, about my patients, their issues, my thoughts. But it's hard to truly know what she would have said. Do either of you still talk to your partners?'

Lanning had planned his opening, using his own feelings and experience to create guidance in the therapy again, re-establish himself as the one with the psychological primacy.

Patrick shifted uncomfortably. He reached out for his cup of coffee and winced, making a low groan and sitting back slowly without the drink. Catherine leaned forward and picked the cup up for him.

Lanning knew they had no interest in talking about the dead, tension was pouring out of them, very much a living thing.

'I notice you seem to be in a lot of physical pain, Patrick. Would you like a break, some painkillers?' Lanning said, immediately wondering if he had breached the limits of his clinical remit. He was the Mind Doctor. He had medical training when he was qualifying to become a psychiatrist but that was a long time ago, and the extent of his diagnostic power was realising someone wasn't feeling one hundred per cent.

'Thanks, doc. I'm okay. I was hit by an idiot who was reading his mobile while riding his bicycle. I was just about to try and answer your question about talking to Maggie...'

Patrick's admission about his injuries seemed to create a space for open dialogue.

'Jesus, Pat. I was so worried, you haven't answered my texts or calls for the last couple of days. I thought you were upset with me or ... something a lot worse. Are you all right? Why didn't you ask for help?'

Patrick tried to smile, although it might have been a grimace, and nodded twice.

'I feel as if I'm talking to Maggie right now', he said, only looking at Lanning and raising his eyebrows.

'What does that mean exactly, Patrick?' Lanning said. He glanced at Catherine and sat back.

'Yes, what does that *actually* mean?' Catherine said. She folded her arms tightly.

'I mean ... I mean that Maggie was always on my case about being more open with my feelings, talking to her about every bloody emotion all day and night, and it became really bloody annoying. She was always getting on my nerves and making me wish...'

Lanning allowed the difficult silence to hang in the room for a few seconds — that had proven to be helpful with other patients in the past. The sound of heavy breathing seemed to suggest there was a lot more anger on its way. He took a deep breath of his own.

'Do you think of Catherine now the way you thought of Maggie, when she asked you how you felt all the time, asking you to be open with your feelings. Do you think of me in that way?'

26

'Do I think of you the same way I thought of my ex-wife?' Patrick said. He laughed mockingly and winced again.

That serves you right, Lanning thought, watching Patrick's eyes close and open.

'She's your *dead* wife, not your ex-wife', Catherine said.

Patrick looked at her quickly then at his coffee cup.

'I'm sorry. I meant to say my wife, my *dead* wife. I do talk to her, and I don't enjoy a lot of the things I hear myself saying to her, and neither one of you are anything like her, completely different. I was completely out of line, and I'm sorry.'

Lanning could have cried out in joy. He had seen the real Patrick Hawton.

Catherine put her hand, carefully, on Patrick's shoulders and rubbed his back. Lanning felt jealous. He longed for human contact again, to feel Jane's soft hands on him.

'I talk to Harry', she said, breathing out slowly. She sipped her coffee. 'Not as much as I did after I was discharged from hospital.'

'Has the nature of your conversations changed?'

'Surely they aren't conversations, doc', Patrick said. He seemed happier now. Lanning preferred the contrite version. 'A conversation has to be a two-way thing, right?'

Lanning smiled. 'Fair enough, let's say dialogues. Have they changed, Catherine?' He pointedly looked away from Patrick. Who needed that sort of semantic interruption in contemplative moments, or ever?

'I guess. I feel a bit odd talking about it, but I suppose it might be helpful. We ... *I* talk about how each day has been, how it might have been different with him there. What I might want to do in the future, that sort of thing.'

'Do you ever talk to him, at him, about the things you didn't like in your relationship *with him*, the things you've always wanted to do but wouldn't have done if he had lived?' Patrick asked.

119

Lanning could feel his mouth tighten. He thought it was a tactless question without any real point except, perhaps, giving Patrick an increased sense of superiority.

'I'm really not sure that's an appropriate que...'

'Would you let *Catherine* decide what she will and won't answer, for god's sake? You always have to be the fucking grown-up. You have no idea what you're even doing here, do you?' Patrick shouted, shooting Lanning a look of rage and dropping his coffee mug.

The room was quiet again. Patrick struggled to his feet and left the study for a few minutes. Neither Catherine or Lanning said a word or made eye contact. The sound of the downstairs toilet flush made Lanning sit further back in his chair. Patrick walked into the room, picked his mug off the floor, placed it on to the table and sat down. He didn't make any groans of pain. Lanning guessed he was probably holding his breath. If only he could have used that discussed and already agreed method before his outburst, but it was too late for any of that. Lanning wanted to drop his pad and pen, leave the study and climb the stairs to his bedroom, pull back the unused duvet and lie next to Jane's place. Perhaps he would shut the door, put his earphones in and listen to their favourite song — Ella Fitzgerald singing *The Very Thought of You*.

'Pat, I think you owe Chris an apology. That was just rudeness for the sake of it', Catherine spoke very slowly. Lanning knew she was looking at him but felt ashamed, as if all of his archaic methods had been stripped away in a flick of the wrist and he was left, naked and shivering, unable to comprehend what he could possibly say that might ever help these two people, or anyone, ever again.

'I'm sorry, doc. I'm in a lot of pain and I don't think I should carry on with the session today.'

Lanning still couldn't raise his head.

26

'Thanks, Pat. Christopher, I think *you* should apologise for attempting to manipulate us into saying what you clearly want to hear.'

Lanning quickly replayed Catherine's last words in his mind. What the hell is she talking about. Where does she get *manipulate* from? Lanning thought, looking at a wall space where Jane's smiling face at a birthday party used to be.

He looked up, unable to hide the look of incredulity which made his face ache.

'I will apologise for seeming judgemental but I don't understand what you mean by using such a strong and accusing word as manipulate.'

He looked at Catherine, who had an unexpectedly disinterested expression. She reminded Lanning of one of his colleagues, who regularly talked over him in review meetings and seemed determined to discredit him.

'We believe you've often tried to ... guide us down a conversational path to fulfil some part of the therapy, as if you're determined to tick various boxes and have enough information to fill the next chapter in your book of some sort.'

Catherine's reference to a written work based on the therapy sessions sent a volt of guilt down Lanning's body. Did they know he was planning a research study? He would be compelled to tell them before it was published but this felt too soon, as if he was robbing a grave.

27

Catherine felt joyous when she arrived home. She put her favourite song on, turned up the volume and danced as if she only had until the end of the track to drain an overdose of energy from her entire body.

When the song was over, she sat down on the middle of the lounge floor and cried until she felt as if she was forcing the sobs. She stood up stretched her arms wide, twisted her waist and touched her toes.

She hadn't used this routine of expressing her emotions since she had been a teenager. It had felt more accessible back then, more natural, something to use in difficult times, and it always helped her, made her feel as if she had the power to know herself fully and draw out any negativity and begin refocusing.

What had been so wrong with Patrick today. He had arrived at the session in the darkest funk, been extremely terse with Lanning and overbearing with her, and he was obviously lying about having been hit by a bike. He looked as if he had been beaten up, and ready to fight again when he was fully recovered.

Catherine had tried to talk to him after the session, walking him home. His every step seemed to be agony but he kept to his story, embellishing it with more lies about how he wouldn't have imagined a relatively slow bike speed could do so much damage when hitting someone on the arm and leg, and that he had taken a fall onto the pavement and that had caused the worst injuries and bruising. All lies. Had his fight been the result of some entry on his version of the deviant list? Had he watched Fight Club and imagined he would be able to transform and fully compartmentalise a side of his character into a Tyler Durden — able to strategise and theorise while getting the shit kicked out of him every night.

She made herself a smoothie and took her deviant list from her bedside table. She added: *lie to Pat, to his face, and smile while he wonders.*

Niamh had sent her a text, an invitation to a party she was holding for their colleagues. Niamh added that she was hoping to finally 'get physical' with Rafe from IT and the party would be her opportunity.

Catherine was still planning to resign from her job, but she hadn't seen her work mates for a long time and the dancing had felt liberating. It might be a chance for her to find some additional deviance, too.

She sent a Niamh a reply: Sounds cool. Rafe? I had no idea! I'll bring a bottle xxx.

The party was three days later. Catherine had tried to contact Patrick, sending a few texts and leaving a voice message, but he hadn't responded. Her concern had become something less although she wondered whether he might have decided pain was part of the process and it made him feel more alive, decided he would take his shirt off again and pick his next opponent. He almost certainly wouldn't be telling her about any of it.

The first rule of Fight Club...

She hadn't been to a party for a long time. Harry preferred intimate dinners with a few friends. She wasn't sure what she preferred and she was anxious about being single again. Was she officially single or would the people from work see her as a version of widowed? She had read about common-law marriage not being legally binding, having been raised to think it was and somehow she and Harry had achieved that status. But they had been a standard couple, a boyfriend and girlfriend, no special title to be conferred upon that, no better than walking home as a teenager, after school, holding hands with some boy she might have liked because of his hair and smile and told her friends about in PE the next day. She didn't want to be thought of as a widow, she felt too young. But it might have been comforting to have something to call her place in the world after Harry's death. She would try to think of a name for it herself — perhaps something like The Leftover?

In the two hours before Niamh's party began, Catherine oscillated between clothing decisions and whether or not she wanted to go out at all or stay at home watching a film, reading a book or redrafting her list.

She felt as if she didn't know anything about her work colleagues anymore, as if the accident, her loss and the waves of grief and change had completely erased her mind and ability to care about the dynamics of her career.

'Cath, my love. Come in, so lovely to see you. You look gorgeous', Niamh said, moving to one side at the front door. Catherine kissed her friend on the cheek, nodded to a couple of Niamh's non-work friends she had met before, and wanted to go home and lock her own front door against any other parties in the future. She wondered whether she should have asked Patrick, but he was probably still recovering and she wasn't ready to show him to her other friends yet — too many questions, too many difficult answers, and it didn't have anything to do with them anyway.

'Rafe isn't here yet', Niamh whispered, sotto voce, into Catherine's ear as they walked to the kitchen. Catherine recognised the song playing in the lounge, she had loved Duran Duran when she was at school, but hadn't understood the lyrics to this track, something about dancing on the valentine. She gave herself a moment to remember what Rafe looked like, smiled and crossed her fingers on both hands for Niamh to see. She couldn't really see the attraction but it didn't have anything to do with her life now and she just wanted her friend to get what she wanted. It did feel a bit pathetic to be holding an entire party with the aim of gaining the interest of one man but dating seemed to be even more difficult these days. She had often felt lucky she had Harry as she listened to her friends bemoaning their single-status lives.

Catherine wanted to ask why Niamh hadn't thought to simply ask Rafe out for a drink, but having her own drink-in-hand and many to come was a lot more important to her right there and then. She would almost certainly get a blow-by-blow report of Niamh's success or failure the following day. She would happily put that irksome task to one side for as long as she could.

She became the centre of attention as more people arrived. Her work colleagues made straight for her, rolling out heartfelt sentiments, which annoyed her for no obvious reasons, about how sorry they were for her loss, how much they had liked Harry, regardless of how little each of them actually knew him, and how brave she was for coming tonight. Her face began to hurt with the smile of thankfulness she pretended. She wished she had made a standard recording of gratitude she could use as soon as she saw one of them approaching — each time, holding her right index to her lips, fixing her grin and pressing play, nodding occasionally for emphasis:

It's been such a hard month ... It's so kind of you to say so ... yes, we must go out for a coffee and chat soon... I'll be in touch ... good to see you ... many thanks...

'Hi Catherine.'

She turned around to see Rafe holding a glass of wine. He was smiling at her and looking as if he had been given a difficult task and wasn't relishing it at all. She wondered whether Niamh had asked him to talk to her as a way of allowing Catherine to declare how wonderful her best friend was and what fantastic parties she held.

'I'm really sorry to hear about your ... partner. I really don't know what to say in situations like this, sorry. How are you doing? That's a stupid question to ask. You must have been asked that a hundred times this evening. Would you like a drink, and an opportunity to talk about something completely different?'

Rafe smiled and dropped his head. He looked up, biting his bottom lip, as if he thought he had made a fool of himself.

Catherine smiled and held out her empty glass.

'I'll have another vodka and tonic, please. And I'd love to talk about anything else. Thanks for asking.'

Rafe was back within a few minutes. Catherine was swaying to a Roxy Music song she couldn't remember the title of.

'What would you like to talk about?' he said, handing her a full glass. He sipped his own topped-up drink. Catherine glanced over his shoulder to see Niamh dancing with another friend from work. She didn't seem distracted by Rafe talking to someone else. Catherine guessed she was considered the Grieving Woman, someone not to be considered a threat by other women, a person who has been removed from the sexual side of life, to be pitied.

'This song. Do you know the title? I know it's by Roxy Music.'

'Love Is The Drug.'

'What was that?'

'That's the title of the song. A lot of people mistake it for one of Bryan Ferry's solo tracks but it's from an album called *Siren*, by Roxy. I think that's the one with Jerry Hall on the front cover ... of the album not the single, this single.'

Rafe pulled a face of fake confusion and made his right index and middle fingers into the shape of a gun which he put against his head. Catherine laughed.

'I only needed the title, but that was certainly interesting. You clearly know a lot about that band.'

Rafe shook his head, smiled again and sipped his drink.

'I seem to retain so much totally irrelevant information. I'm fascinated by research, small details. It's a shame I didn't spend as much time on my degree', he said.

27

There were a few moments of silence between them but it wasn't uncomfortable for Catherine. She danced to the last part of the song, looked at Rafe doing the same and thought how much better looking he was than she had remembered.

'Shall we get drunk and talk about the small details of life', she asked, leaning into him, her lips close to his left ear, able to smell his deodorant.

He nodded, saluted and took both of their empty glasses to the kitchen, returning as a new song began to play. Niamh was watching Rafe now. She caught Catherine's eye and half-smiled as if she could barely contain signs of her increasing anxiety.

Catherine recognised the song title this time: *Poison Arrow*.

28

Patrick could still see some green and yellow faded traces of the bruise around his right eye. He had ignored calls and texts for a few days and cancelled his appearance at the shared therapy session that week. Catherine hadn't tried to contact him for some time and only Celia had knocked at his front door.

'I haven't heard anything from you for a couple of weeks. Are you all right? Is that a bruise?'

Patrick didn't want to see his sister or talk about his face, he was ashamed of himself, of how easily Leigh Evans could still manage to humiliate and hurt him, and how he had alienated both Lanning and Catherine. He didn't really care about Lanning's feelings too much, although he did need him to validate his plans and behaviour. The man was paid to listen and understand. But to think of how upset Catherine might be made him want to punch a wall until his hand was shattered into pieces. He had become lonely.

Celia was better than loneliness.

'I don't get it. Why would you need a list like that? It doesn't sound very helpful. Have you spoken to your doctor, your psychiatrist doctor, about it?' Celia said. She looked tired, her eyes were puffy, as if she had been crying. She picked up her mug of tea and put it down again. Patrick noticed her hand was trembling.

'What aren't you telling me, Pat? What really caused your injuries? Did you hit someone or do something to yourself? Please talk to me. Do you still ... do you want to die?'

Patrick saw tears in his sister's eyes and realised he had completely missed them before. She *had* been crying when she arrived.

'Die? What on earth makes you say that? How did you know about my list?'

28

Celia wiped her face and drank tea. Patrick wondered whether he should say more immediately, accuse her of prying into his personal life, but decided to allow his sister time to explain. How could she possibly have seen a list he had stored on his mobile phone?

'I think you must have sent me a text by accident. It was a list of weird things you were thinking about doing. You called it your *afterlife desires (revised)*.'

Patrick clenched his jaw. He meant to send that to Catherine. He must have forgotten to wear his reading glasses, seen the capitalised C and pressed send.

'That was a poor joke, a moment of feeling down and grabbing your attention, a skit on what you do for a living. It was in truly terrible taste. I'm really sorry, sister of mine.'

Celia breathed out and widened her eyes.

'That was in *appalling* taste. Jesus wept. I've been terrified about coming over and finding you dead. Patrick, please don't ever do anything like that again. Are you *really* all right? Are you still talking to your doctor?'

'True. Sorry. Promise. Yes. Yes.'

Patrick smiled. Celia gave him a rueful stare back.

'Are those one word answers an attempt at another skit on advertising and its vacuous attempts to dumb everything down?'

'Yes', Patrick said, in a robotic voice.

Celia picked up the cushion next to her leg and threw it at him. He caught it and slammed his face into it, making a pig squeal which had always made his sister laugh. Simple things matter, he thought.

Dean Clift lived eight miles away from Patrick. He had posted a recent photograph of himself on Facebook, standing next to a road sign, one of his meaty hands pointing at the sign, the other at a house behind it. The post read: *Nu home, nu start!*

129

The house number was clear, and Google provided a distance and easiest route to follow. Patrick was determined to do things differently this time — no surveillance, no plan, just a random journey culminating in either failure, which would be returning home without any contact, or the success of confronting this Ultimate Moron and using the purity of spontaneous shock and awe to make his point about the past and its implications very clear.

He wondered if Leigh Evans might find out about the meeting, after the fact, from another Facebook post, and wonder if it was Patrick, ready this time.

Probably not, although he still knew how to get the better of Patrick, he was also still an idiot. He would almost certainly think it was the work of someone able to 'handle themselves' — not a wimp like *Hawthorn*.

Lanning had sent Patrick a few texts, more than a few, fifteen, and one voice message, asking him whether he would be fit enough to return to the following session, that it was essential for them all to talk through *recent events* and discuss the best way forward. It sounded desperate to Patrick, he hadn't replied yet.

He knew what he had to do to move forward: settle things with Catherine, make her forgive him, and settle things with Clift, giving himself agency to forget *everything* he used to be.

When Patrick decided to kill Dean Clift he chose his father's old driving gloves to cover any skin traces and fingerprints and a carving knife, carried inside a supermarket plastic bag Maggie had borrowed from her mother and not returned. Patrick had imagined what stabbing someone, or being stabbed himself, might feel like, but didn't have any idea how he might feel afterwards.

Would it be over quickly, without some last quip available to let flap around the dying man's ears as he crumpled into a void?

He hadn't planned to travel to see Dean Clift on any particular day, he chose a sunny one because it filled him with a confidence that everything would be all right.

He recognised Clift's car from the Facebook post and guessed, correctly, as it was only 7.30 in the morning, the Ultimate Moron would still be going through his morning clichés — shower, shave...

Patrick waited some distance away from Clift's home. He looked at some of the other houses in the cul-de-sac; they were the same design and he was happy he didn't live in one of them. As he glanced back to Clift's pillar-box red front door, he noticed it open, and there he was, the worst of the lot, kissing and waving a goodbye to his wife and daughter. Clift was wearing an ill-fitting suit and, what Patrick hadn't been able to see in any of the Facebook posts, Clift had lost most of the hair from the top of his head. That made Patrick breathe in deeply and smile. *That* alone was a type of justice, Clift had spent hours applying wet-look hair gel and preening his mullet style in the toilets at school. He had also worn skin-tight Farah trousers and white socks in those days, always tucking his Pringle sweater in and pushing his chest out.

But he was now at least thirty pounds too heavy for any legwear which didn't have an elasticated waistband. Regardless of baldness and weight gain, Clift looked happy, as if he was content with his copycat house and his little family of joy. He didn't deserve any of it and Patrick knew he had to feel helpless, terrified, wild thoughts flashing threw his empty head in his last moments: *why is this happening to me?*

He should feel what Patrick had felt and never be allowed to do anything like it again. A creature like Clift could never really change. Patrick was doing the world a service.

He followed Clift for a few miles, staying a couple of cars back. The journey didn't take long. Clift was an estate agent. His office was full of desks occupied by much younger people already on their telephones, looking at their laptop screens, most of them with expressions of false bonhomie. None of them even looked up when Clift walked in. Patrick wondered if he might be in charge, the dreaded and hated boss, but he soon sat down behind another standard desk, opened his laptop and picked up his phone. He was a drone.

How completely depressing your life is, Patrick thought. I'll be doing you a favour.

Patrick was getting bored of waiting for Clift to finish work. He thought about taking a chance and walking into the estate agency, sitting at Clift's desk, engaging him in conversation about a particular home, asking if they could visit it immediately and dealing with him when they arrived. But that was full of risks — being seen by his colleagues, he didn't have any disguise, was the main one. It was a terrible idea. He would have to wait until, hopefully, lunchtime. But what if Dean ate in the office break room, at his desk or went out with his co-workers? This entire day was supposed to be over with quickly. It was fast becoming another surveillance task, another potential Leigh Evans' beating down for him. What if one of the many calls Clift had made that morning was to his old school friend, double-checking Patrick's current physical description and car type?

Clift closed his laptop and picked up his briefcase. He spoke to the receptionist, who handed him something in an envelope, and walked out of the office.

Patrick's heart gained speed. He breathed in and out slowly, ignoring everything but Clift's car. He must be on his way to showing a house, his own property was in the other direction.

The sun was in Patrick's eyes, he unfolded his windscreen visor and reached out for his sunglasses. He thought of Catherine and of turning his car around and going to visit her. But he couldn't live with that — capitulating to the easiest option again, that was Maggie's way, the part of himself he despised.

28

Clift indicated right and came to a stop mid-way along a road full of new-looking houses. Patrick didn't know the name of building materials but the bricks were the colour of dry sand. The sunlight made them look only just finished. He parked on the corner of the street.

Clift got out of his car, stretched, finished his sandwich, took a drink from his bottle of water and checked his mobile phone.

Patrick looked around, at the streetlights and house facades; there didn't appear to be any CCTV cameras, and he couldn't see any residents or other cars.

This was a new housing estate. Clift was parked outside a show home.

Patrick put his driving gloves on and reached behind his seat for the plastic bag. He found the blunt edge of the knife and slowly brought the bag on to his lap, keeping his eyes on Clift, who had propped himself against his car, still looking at his mobile phone.

The handle of the knife felt slippery even with leather gloves on; sweat was growing all over him. Patrick closed his eyes tightly and blew three furious puffs. He opened his door and got out and up quickly, catching his right foot on the kerb.

As he walked towards Clift, as casually as he could manage, he expected this Ultimate Moron of Morons to look up, take a moment to focus on his face, then perhaps either smile, thinking Patrick was his client, or reach into his car for an even bigger knife after realising who was on his way.

'Hi, can I help you?' Clift's voice was as familiar to Patrick as his own. So many years had passed and yet he felt as vulnerable now as he had ever done at school. He had the attention of the one person on the planet who he had tried, and failed day after day at school, to avoid. 'Are you lost?'

Patrick looked over his shoulder, half-expecting, and hoping, to see someone else behind him, that he was invisible.

'Are you all right?' Clift's voice sounded concerned.

How is it possible *he* would have the capacity to sound concerned about *me,* Patrick thought. He's evil.

He tightened his grip on the plastic bag, the side of the knife bumped on his thighs. The weight of it reminded him he was in charge of the scene.

Now Clift was walking towards him. He was coming for him.

'Can I help you?' he said. Clift was offering *help.*

Then Clift was standing in front of him. He was smiling, and it seemed genuine.

'I'm Dean. What's your name?'

'Patrick ... Patrick Hawton. Hawton not Hawthorn.'

Clift's smile dropped quickly. He stared into space for a few moments, then back at Patrick.

'I thought that was you. Patrick ... Hawton, wow, this is a huge surprise. It's been such a long time. How are you? Are you looking to buy one of these houses? I'm an estate agent now. I could arrange...'

'I'm here to kill you.' Patrick heard himself say the words, but they didn't sound real. They reminded him of scripted lines from a Western — him as mysterious stranger, having ridden into town, arriving at the one and only saloon to avenge the death of a friend.

'What was that?'

Clift was smiling again.

'You ruined my life, at school, ruined it. You and Evans, and the dead weightlifter.'

Clift's eyed widened. He looked back at his car, at Patrick's hands, and at the plastic bag.

'I'm sorry, Patrick. I'm *really* sorry. This is a big surprise. I didn't expect...'

And Clift did look *really* sorry. Patrick was waiting for his face to twist into the same nasty grin he had at school — malicious, desperate to impress the other teenage hyenas, the girls Patrick liked but who laughed along with Clift — relishing the terror he could provoke in those weaker than him. But he looked contrite, as if he meant it.

'I was awful at school, a bastard. I'm sure I emotionally scarred a lot of people. We all did. I understand why you feel the way you do, but I've changed. I'm a lay minister now, at my local church, Saint Nicholas. I work in the evenings and at weekends, to help kids like I was, the ones who get left behind, abuse alcohol, other drugs too, like I did...'

'That's all very religious and God-loving of you, congratulations on your new found goodness. But you need to pay for what you did back *then*. You don't get to wipe away the past as if it never mattered.'

Clift had said he understood how Patrick felt. Lanning said that a lot. Was he so easy to understand, were his motivations, responses and reasons so childish and transparent that even a moron such as Clift could understand?

'How can I make amends to you, Patrick?'

Patrick didn't know how to answer. He had become calm and cold. His legs were getting tired and his heart had slowed. He didn't feel like killing anyone now. He wanted to go home.

He felt his mobile phone vibrate.

'Can I buy you a cup of tea? You don't look well', Clift said. He reached out to put his hand on Patrick's arm.

'Keep your paw off me', Patrick shouted. He stepped back and plunged his dominant hand into the plastic bag, taking the handle of the knife, after accidentally gripping the blade first.

'Okay, okay. That's understandable', Clift said. He held up his hands in surrender, glanced at Patrick's bag and moved backwards.

'*Why* did you do that shit to me all the time? *Why* did you all hate me so much?'

Clift breathed out heavily and sat down on the kerb. He rubbed his hands together.

'I had a heart attack a few years ago', he said.

Patrick shook his head, surprised to hear something as serious as that from a contemporary, then annoyed Clift hadn't died.

'I really thought I was going to die. I had been abusing alcohol and other drugs for ages, people too. I deserved to feel that way, and I probably should have died. I won't make excuses for why I did all of that. I was a bastard and it made me feel better to hurt other people.'

'But *why?*'

'If I start explaining it to you, you might think I'm trying to excuse myself. I did those things to you, Patrick, that was *me then*. You deserve my best to try and make up for some of that. Is there any way I can help you to heal?'

Patrick took his hand out of the bag and sat on the kerb, a few feet from Clift. He kept the bag close, still not fully trusting all of the God Forgives talk.

'Tell me, why me?'

'I don't know where to begin', Clift whispered.

'Why me?' Patrick shouted, standing up, feeling his hand gripping the plastic bag, the blade cutting into the glove leather. 'Fucking remember why.'

Clift stood up. He looked at his hands, brushed his jacket and shrugged.

'Because it was easy. You never fought back.'

Patrick didn't know what to say. He wanted to hit Clift, say something that would emotionally crush him, question his faith, perhaps bring on another heart attack. But all he could manage were a few broken sounds.

He turned away and began to walk back to his car.

'I am sorry, Patrick. Truly. I think God's forgiven me. He loves all of us. I hope you can forgive me too', Clift called out.

Patrick drove away without looking back. He stopped next to a field and stared at some cows.

'God forgives. He loves us.'

28

He punched the steering wheel. The car horn burst out. His hand was aching, but he needed to feel the pain. He needed to feel the rage. He punched the dashboard, the windscreen, his legs, his face, over and over until his nose was bleeding. He blinked and saw Maggie sitting next to him. She was crying, staring at him with complete despair.

He felt his phone vibrate again. He pulled it out of his jacket pocket. Catherine had left him three voice messages.

'All I need is *your* forgiveness', he said, as he began to listen to the first message.

'Hi Patrick. This is Catherine. I feel terrible. I did something really stupid and I would love to see you and talk it through. Please call or text me. Thanks.'

29

Lanning knew this would be the last session. Both Catherine and Patrick looked ashen. Patrick had more facial bruising and Catherine looked thinner. Where would he even begin from — crack a couple of jokes or do an impersonation? Had they been in love and fallen out of it now?

'How are you both?'

That seemed like a broad and caring question. Inoffensive enough to draw one of them out, perhaps.

If they had asked him the same thing, he would have told them he had resigned from the hospital, decided to give up psychiatry. That he had spent most of the previous two days in his attic, looking through his shared history with Jane: her Dunlop tennis pumps, hardened by mud and humidity, water damaged novels, watching the sunlight creep through a small hole in the roof, a gap from a detached tile, and weeping, screaming with no sounds, while he held a woolly hat and scarf Jane had been wearing on their first date. He would have told them they were the only reason he was still alive.

Catherine was clearly finding eye contact difficult. Her eyes looked red, as if she hadn't slept for days and rubbed her face raw, overwhelmed by fatigue and the frustration of insomnia.

Patrick looked defeated. He was sitting up very straight in his chair, like a man awaiting a sentence of many years for a particularly awful crime. His unshaven face had healing cuts and oddly shaped bruises all over it. They looked like a row of coins had been pressed into his skin. Had he joined a boxing club or something to do with martial arts — would it be presumptuous and inconsequential to ask him? Lanning decided against asking. He was beyond worrying about the smaller details of the therapy now. They were able to cope without his observations.

'I'm planning a holiday soon', Lanning said. It wasn't true but he wanted their attention. It worked. They both focused on him.

'Where to?' Catherine asked. She smiled at him. He wanted to cry again. Such a small gesture of kindness but it felt like one of *the* things of life in that moment.

'I'm not really sure, perhaps one of the places I visited with my wife, hunting for the wonder of memories.'

'Perhaps you can create some new memories.'

He looked at Catherine and felt as if she was his biggest success. She would survive whatever was bothering her now, all travails still to come. He had helped her find her inner strength again.

If Lanning had planned to go anywhere, he would have chosen Florence — although he would never have returned there without Jane. His fondest memories were their walks over the Ponte Vecchio, alongside the River Arno and through the Renaissance streets, past the Uffizi, looking up at Il Duomo, the beauty of natural discovery around each corner.

They had made love in the dry spring hills overlooking the city while visiting a small church called Santa Maria della Croce. Jane had laughed guiltily about the sacrilege, that God had been watching them. Lanning said God would understand, would probably have looked away, and that He was supposed to *be Love*.

Lanning wanted to live and die there. He wanted one more day with Jane in that memory. One more kiss, touching her face. One more minute to tell her how much he totally loved her.

'Are you going to be away for a while?' Patrick said. He sounded annoyed, as if he wanted to ask Lanning to stay but couldn't bring himself to admit any needs or vulnerability. Perhaps this was the biggest failure and success of the shared therapy — the two patients had moved further away from him and closer to each other.

'I'm not sure. It will probably be a short journey.'

'Is there anything in particular you'd advise us to think about while you're gone?'

Catherine leaned forward to hear the answer. She looked different now. She looked like Jane.

'Just be kind to yourselves. That might sound boring and simplistic, but it's so hard to achieve and know how to do. You work really well together. You've come such a long way already.'

Lanning walked them to the front door. He shook Patrick's hand, nodding and smiling at him. Patrick nodded in return, looking pensive. Lanning was about to do the same with Catherine. She leaned in, hugged him tightly and kissed his cheek.

'Take care of yourself, too', she whispered to him.

He took the coffee tray to the kitchen, rinsed the mugs and biscuit plate and put them in the dishwasher. Then he returned to the study and put the chairs and table back in their original places. He tidied his desk and typed his session notes. He sent the shared therapy file to one of his colleagues at the hospital with a note: Alan, please read this and look in on Catherine and Patrick when you can. Many thanks. Christopher (Dr C Lanning).

As he changed all of his clothes, having found his wedding suit in the attic, spending over an hour brushing, steaming and ironing it, he remembered the morning he got married, how his hands were shaking so much he couldn't knot his tie correctly. Jane had taken care of that. She had always taken care.

He polished his shoes and combed his hair, it needed cutting. Then he picked up his favourite of all of Jane's photographs, a black and white image of her sitting on Brighton beach, nine years ago, looking out to the English Channel, her left hand shielding her eyes from the sun, as if she was watching forever.

Lanning had used his hospital keys to gather enough Diazepam and Clozapine for his journey. He sat on the study sofa, next to Jane's wedding dress, her Brighton beach photo sat on top of the dress, and emptied the eight blister packs into his hands. He had opened the bottle of Champagne given to him by his colleagues to celebrate the ten years in his position at the hospital. It had gathered a lot of dust since. He poured two glasses and clinked them together.

'To our home', he said to Jane's image. He kissed her face through the frame and took all of the pills in three parts, eventually falling asleep to the crescendo of Samuel Barber's *Adagio for Strings*.

30

Catherine told Patrick everything she could remember about what had happened between she and Rafe at Niamh's party and how bad she felt about the destruction of her best friendship.

'She said I hadn't been in love with Harry, that I had been pretending because I was scared of being alone. Do you think that might have been true?' Catherine said the words quickly. Patrick touched her hand. He looked beaten up again, new cuts and his nose was bruised this time.

Fight clubbing? Catherine wondered.

'Niamh's angry with you. She probably didn't mean any of that, and it's a completely uninformed opinion. She wasn't living with the two of you.'

'I don't even remember kissing Rafe. I didn't want to kiss Rafe, or anyone. We were dancing and drinking and laughing. I think I fell asleep on his shoulder during *Careless Whisper*. I never liked that song much.'

Patrick laughed.

'Very school disco', he said.

Catherine rolled her eyes.

'I think we kissed, a bit. Niamh made it sound as though she caught us having wild sex. She went nuts. It doesn't matter what happened with Rafe. I've screwed up things with my best friend. I quit my job after that argument.'

Patrick had been sipping his peppermint tea. He gulped his mouthful down.

'For real?'

'Yep. I'm done there. I haven't got it in me to go back. I realised I haven't enjoyed the job for a long time. Things ... after Harry, changed for me. At least I won't have to endure seeing Niamh, or Rafe.'

'Good for you. What are you going to do next?'

Catherine shrugged. 'Take some time to consider things. I might travel. I don't know. Are you all right? You look a bit tired.'

Patrick nodded and gave a thumbs-up.

Catherine spent three days thinking about her future, trying, unsuccessfully, to make up with Niamh and realising she hadn't done a single thing on her deviance list. Rafe wasn't a deviant act, just a stupid one.

She looked through her current choices, drank wine and decided to take on one of her *goodwill deviances* first. She had trouble putting one of her trainers on. Perhaps it was the third glass of wine but it just as easily might be that her feet had swollen on this humid day.

She walked to the local supermarket slowly, looking left and right many times before crossing any roads.

'The first one I see hits the jackpot', she whispered to herself.

There was a young woman sitting on the pavement outside the supermarket. She had placed a small paper cup in front of her shoes.

A sign was next to the cup: Please give anything you can spare. I'm very hungry. God bless you.

'Hello', Catherine said. She knew she was swaying. 'Are you *really* hungry?'

'Yeah, I am. Why?'

Catherine realised she had sounded patronising. She was thinking about her next sentence, clearly taking too long to reply. The young woman was looking around her, at her hands, then beginning to roll a cigarette.

'I would like to get you some food, anything you like. I brought a bag with me.'

She pulled a plastic bag from her pocket, Patrick had given it to her for her wet bicycle seat. She waved it open wide.

143

'Shall we go in and fill this for you?'

'You're drunk, mate', the woman said. She lit her cigarette and nodded at passers-by, most of whom said they couldn't help her.

'I'm just tired. What would you like? I'll get you anything you like. Would you like a sandwich, some crisps, a pudding?'

Catherine made herself stand up straight and still. She was both drunk and tired.

'It's okay, thanks. You should probably go home, mate.'

Catherine looked into the supermarket. There were two fridge cabinets inside the entry doors.

'I'll be right back. Don't go anywhere', she said

The young woman shrugged and took a long drag on her cigarette, blowing smoke out of the side of her mouth. She yawned.

Catherine rubbed her eyes and flexed her mouth, which now felt drier than she could remember. She walked into the supermarket and noticed rows of chilled bottled water. She reached out for the nearest one, turning it over twice to find the price. She was too thirsty to wait. She twisted the cap off, immediately feeling a gush of the water across her hand and wrist. The surprise made her drop the bottle, which rolled into another aisle.

'Sodding sparkling.'

The sandwiches all seemed so elaborate — salmon and mayonnaise with chives, ham and Stilton, beef with horseradish and pickle...

Who eats those, she thought, pushing past each selection.

Eventually she saw what looked like the last packet of plain cheddar cheese and salad. She picked it up, found a bottle of still water and some ready salted crisps and began walking back to the entry doors.

She looked out, at the young woman, and was about to call to her, showing the goods of her success, ticking something off

30

her list. Harry would be proud of her for getting on with life, helping herself and others.

'We're going to call the police. We need you to sit down and wait for them, please', said a tall, broad man. He was bald, wearing a cheap-looking navy blue jacket, a white shirt and a clip-on blue tie. He was obviously physically strong and had the look of a nightclub bouncer.

The office door opened. A woman, also wearing a suit, more expensive looking, walked in. She sat at a desk and opened a laptop, brought up the template of a form and typed in a few details, then she turned her chair and looked at Catherine.

'I'm Rebecca, the store manager. I need your name, please.'

Catherine had been standing against the wall opposite Rebecca's desk, having tried to leave the office twice and been blocked. The broad man was a few feet in front of her. She sat back down and looked at Rebecca.

'I would like a glass of water, please. Then you can have my name.'

'Would you be able to get a glass of water, please, John.'

The broad man nodded and opened the office door. He returned seconds later.

'Thanks', Catherine said. Her mouth was still so dry and she felt hot.

'My name's Catherine Stannard. Why am I being kept in here?'

'We're waiting for the police to arrive. It's our policy to always prosecute shoplifters', Rebecca said. She typed Catherine's name onto the form. 'You took some water, some sandwiches and some crisps, is that right?'

Catherine was about to nod, but stopped herself.

'I'm not saying anything. I was drunk and I don't remember anything about that.'

'That's fine, Catherine. We have CCTV footage and our security officers saw you.'

The heat in Catherine's face was increasing. She looked around the office, the light orange walls were made of breeze blocks and virtually bare, apart from a Health and Safety poster. Catherine thought it might look akin to a prison cell. She sipped some more of the water and looked at her feet. The lace in one of her trainers was open.

As she looked up she saw Harry sitting in the corner next to the office door. He was slowly shaking his head and the look of disappointment on his face made Catherine feel as if she had failed throughout her life, that she had no chance of redemption.

'I'm sorry. I'm really sorry. Please don't think that way about me. I can make all of this better. I can do everything better from now on', she said, but Harry kept looking disappointed and shaking his head; his right cheek was heavily scarred.

'Try and calm down, Catherine. The police will be here soon. You can explain everything you want when they arrive. Okay?'

'I'm sorry. Please stop looking at me that way. I didn't know any of this was going to happen. I was trying to be a good person. Please forgive me for making a mistake, just a small mistake. Please just say it's all right.'

Catherine didn't remember shouting or standing up.

She woke up and looked at a different young woman sitting next to her, who was wearing a green uniform, *paramedic* was printed on to her epaulettes. Catherine glanced around, quickly realising she was inside an ambulance.

'How are you feeling now, Catherine?'

'Okay, I think. How did I get...'

'You fainted. We're taking you to the hospital to be checked out. Okay?'

Catherine tried to sit up, but felt too dizzy.

'Do the police know I'm here? I'm supposed to be talking to them about the shopping.'

The paramedic smiled. 'I think that's okay now. The manager said she wasn't going to need them. She called us.'

'Could someone call my father, please.'
'We'll do that in a while. We need to get you checked out first. Okay?'
'Okay.'
Catherine lay back, then looked overhead and around the ambulance for any sign of Harry. But he was gone, and she was going to the hospital again. Would Lanning be waiting for her there, shaking his head as Harry had done? Perhaps Patrick would do the same — all of them so disappointed in her.

'I'm thinking of getting another dog, maybe from the rescue centre', Catherine's father said. He poured himself a glass of pineapple juice, bit into a croissant and smiled at her. Catherine knew he was probably desperate to ask her how she had come to be back at the hospital, they hadn't talked much the previous evening. Catherine had called him, asking for a lift and could she stay with him for a couple of days. He had sounded surprised but instantly agreed. She had kissed him goodnight as soon as they arrived home and gone to her childhood bedroom, falling asleep within minutes of getting into bed and only waking when she heard the kettle boiling in her parents' bedroom for early morning cups of tea.

'What sort are you looking for?'
Catherine was happy to be thinking of mundane things, the familiarity of other lives close to hers. She held her coffee mug with both hands, clearing her throat which was very sore.

'Something friendly, a sheepdog or an Irish Setter?'
'Nice. That sounds like a really good idea.'
'I miss having one on a walk. It feels like something's wrong being there on my own.'

Catherine knew her father's last statement was as close to a direct question about her mental health as he would get.

'I'm okay, dad. I promise. I had a bad day and I must have missed a meal, had low blood sugar, who knows. Thanks for picking me up and letting me stay.'

'No need for any thanks, lovely, not ever. This will always be your home. It would be great if you stayed for a while. You could help me choose the new dog?'

Catherine leaned over the garden room table and hugged her father.

She stayed at her parents' home for three more days. Her father seemed less interested in the idea of choosing a new pet, enjoying walks with Catherine and asking her, twice, if she would consider moving back into the family home permanently.

'It would mean you could have the security of your house sale money in your bank account, and take all the time you need to decide what you actually want to do next, a new job, go back into education, travel a bit, whatever you fancy', he said.

Catherine knew he was making good sense but she missed the independence of her own home, and she missed Patrick. He had sent her a few checking-in texts, but they hadn't spoken for almost a week. She sent him a short message: Hey, Silent Bob, you okay? Fancy meeting for a coffee and chat? Xx.

31

'But you *wanted* to kill him?' Catherine said, holding her mug of coffee to the side of her mouth, as if it were an exhibit, something to make a point clear.

Patrick nodded and breathed in and out deeply.

'I wanted to but I couldn't go through with it, I couldn't ever do that. He was apologising and seemed so pathetic, so small now. He had moved on from that time and was trying to be a different and better person. He knew he had done bad things. But I have too. Evans probably still deserves to suffer and learn, but it doesn't matter and that's not my concern. It's all better forgotten about. I shouldn't have tried to go back. That was the mistake, thinking I could change anything. I think I miss Maggie more than I had realised. I was blaming her for everything that wasn't right about *me* about the way I *feel*. But it was all about the grief I *was* feeling. Anyway, I think it's over now. I just want to be honest with you.'

Catherine stood up, looked around Patrick's lounge, out of the window and sat back down.

'Why aren't there any photos of Maggie around? I've never seen her.'

Patrick opened his mobile phone and found the last photo he had taken of her, a day out at Stonehenge, after realising neither of them had visited it before. Catherine took the phone.

'She was beautiful', she said, handing it back and holding Patrick's fingertips for a moment.

'I thought I needed to start fresh. I thought I couldn't do that with her watching me all the time from the images of our life together. It felt like an infection I had to recover from, all those experiences I remembered as being a chore, but that was the good stuff and I blew it all away. That was another part of it, thinking I hadn't ever loved her or needed her. But I did, I really did. I guess happiness is a strong word, something you feel you were in retrospect.'

Patrick began to cry. Catherine sat next to him and put her arm around his waist and her head on his shoulder. She cried too.

Patrick looked at the Margaret Atwood books on the top bookshelf to his right and thought of his dead partner; how those books would probably never be read again, how Maggie's DNA would cling to the pages until they became browned and disintegrated. History and fiction crumbling away. The past and its interpretations.

'Would you like to come away with me?' Catherine asked, placing another mug of tea in front of Patrick.

He looked up quickly.

'I'm not suggesting we elope, don't worry. I mean, come away for a journey of some kind?'

Patrick sipped his tea and nodded slowly.

'That sounds like a great idea. When?'

'Tomorrow morning.'

'Will I need my passport?'

'Bring it, just in case.'

They sat opposite each other and smiled for a while.

Patrick called Celia that evening. He hadn't done that for months, possibly years.

'Are you all right?' she said, as soon as she picked up the call.

Patrick couldn't help imagining she might decide to pitch that exact question as *the* tagline for an emerging product, perhaps a new and improved analgesic.

'Fine, sis. I wanted to tell you I'm going away for a while. Not sure where, just a break some place, or places. I'll stay in contact.'

Celia didn't answer.

'Sister of mine?' Patrick used his Psychedelic Furs vocal impersonation, drawling the question mark after the three

31

words out as much like Richard Butler as he could manage until his throat began to ache. When they were children Celia had pretended she liked the band, even though Patrick knew she only listened to *Pretty in Pink* on repeat.

'Why, why now?' Where to? Are you going on your own?' she said. Patrick thought she was crying.

'I need to. I feel as if I haven't really begun to start getting through the loss of Maggie. I need to get my head straight. I'll be fine. I'm not sure where I'm going yet, but wherever I go, there will always be an advert to remind me of you.'

Celia laughed. Patrick did too. It seemed like old times.

'Are you going alone?'

'With Catherine.'

'Catherine ... *the* Catherine?'

'Yes, *the* Catherine. And no, it's not about sex. It's a genuine connection, whatever that might mean or lead to.'

'Okay, well, I hope you have a good time and feel better. If you need anything at all, call or text me. Probably text me first, that always gets my attention.'

'I understand, sis. I will get your attention if I need it. And thank you for helping me, even when I was too stupid to see it. I'm off to a better place. You can use that in a campaign.'

'That's a terrible pitch. It sounds like the tagline for a funeral directors. Love you, bro.'

'Love you too, sister of mine. You'll always be pretty in pink.'

Catherine looked back at her car, as if it might leave without them, at the extra-large and very full rucksack behind the driver's seat, and waited for Patrick to answer his front door. She had stayed up until after midnight deciding what was essential for a journey: lots of warm clothing, definitely, a nice evening dress, definitely not.

'Good morning, fellow traveller', Patrick said, opening the door quickly, grinning, looking happier than Catherine had ever seen him.

They packed the car, decided to split the driving between them into two-hour stints, and put the radio on. There was a male French voice singing, energetic and impassioned.

'I know this one. It's called *Le temps*. I saw it in a film, with Maggie, one of the first we saw together. I think the lyrics are about love and time passing', Patrick said. 'Where to first?'

'Not sure. Let's just start driving and see where we end.'

FICTION

Put simply, we publish great stories. Whether it's literary or popular, a gentle tale or a pulsating thriller, the connecting theme in all Roundfire fiction titles is that once you pick them up you won't want to put them down.
If you have enjoyed this book, why not tell other readers by posting a review on your preferred book site.

Recent bestsellers from Roundfire are:

The Bookseller's Sonnets
Andi Rosenthal

The Bookseller's Sonnets intertwines three love stories with a tale of religious identity and mystery spanning five hundred years and three countries.

Paperback: 978-1-84694-342-3 ebook: 978-184694-626-4

Birds of the Nile
An Egyptian Adventure
N.E. David

Ex-diplomat Michael Blake wanted a quiet birding trip up the Nile – he wasn't expecting a revolution.

Paperback: 978-1-78279-158-4 ebook: 978-1-78279-157-7

Blood Profit$
The Lithium Conspiracy
J. Victor Tomaszek, James N. Patrick, Sr.

The blood of the many for the profits of the few… *Blood Profit$* will take you into the cigar-smoke-filled room where American policy and laws are really made.

Paperback: 978-1-78279-483-7 ebook: 978-1-78279-277-2

The Burden
A Family Saga
N.E. David

Frank will do anything to keep his mother and father apart. But he's carrying baggage – and it might just weigh him down …

Paperback: 978-1-78279-936-8 ebook: 978-1-78279-937-5

The Cause
Roderick Vincent
The second American Revolution will be a
fire lit from an internal spark.
Paperback: 978-1-78279-763-0 ebook: 978-1-78279-762-3

Don't Drink and Fly
The Story of Bernice O'Hanlon: Part One
Cathie Devitt
Bernice is a witch living in Glasgow. She loses her way
in her life and wanders off the beaten track looking for the
garden of enlightenment.
Paperback: 978-1-78279-016-7 ebook: 978-1-78279-015-0

Gag
Melissa Unger
One rainy afternoon in a Brooklyn diner, Peter Howland
punctures an egg with his fork. Repulsed, Peter pushes
the plate away and never eats again.
Paperback: 978-1-78279-564-3 ebook: 978-1-78279-563-6

The Master Yeshua
The Undiscovered Gospel of Joseph
Joyce Luck
Jesus is not who you think he is. The year is 75 CE. Joseph
ben Jude is frail and ailing, but he has a prophecy to fulfil …
Paperback: 978-1-78279-974-0 ebook: 978-1-78279-975-7

On the Far Side, There's a Boy
Paula Coston

Martine Haslett, a thirty-something 1980s woman, plays hard on the fringes of the London drag club scene until one night which prompts her to sign up to a charity. She writes to a young Sri Lankan boy, with consequences far and long.

Paperback: 978-1-78279-574-2 ebook: 978-1-78279-573-5

Tuareg
Alberto Vazquez-Figueroa

With over 5 million copies sold worldwide, *Tuareg* is a classic adventure story from best-selling author Alberto Vazquez-Figueroa, about honour, revenge and a clash of cultures.

Paperback: 978-1-84694-192-4

Readers of ebooks can buy or view any of these bestsellers by clicking on the live link in the title. Most titles are published in paperback and as an ebook. Paperbacks are available in traditional bookshops. Both print and ebook formats are available online.

Find more titles and sign up to our readers' newsletter at
www.collectiveinkbooks.com/fiction